Jimmie

Jim Valentine

Table of Contents

Dedication

To Jimmie's memory and all his friends and supporters.

Acknowledgements

The loving support and encouragement from my longtime spouse Judith Valentine.

Chapter 1

I

╫╫╫

If modern romance is a firework display with screaming rockets, glittering climaxes, and a final deafening bang, then Jim and Judy were the damp match that refused to strike. No soaring crescendos, no impassioned declarations, and not a single swoon-worthy flourish. Instead, they approached courtship with the same cautious indifference one might reserve for public transit schedules: functional, faintly tiresome, and ideally someone else's problem.

Judy Gleason stood at an imperious five feet eight, a height that forced nearby men to reconsider their spines and their self-worth in quick succession. She was, in the clinical sense, attractive, though more in the way a well-designed bridge is attractive: sturdy, elegant, and built to endure storms without fuss. Her beauty was purely incidental, the unintended byproduct of sound genetics and a longstanding refusal to pander. While her contemporaries fluttered their eyelashes and feigned delight at things they barely understood, Judy conjugated Latin verbs with the ferocity of a Vatican grammarian and treated ringing telephones like small, insolent dogs.

Jim Valentine, by contrast, moved through life with the solemn dignity of a grandfather clock: tall, precise, and faintly bewildered to still be running. At six feet four, he enjoyed the kind of altitude that made people assume he knew what he was doing. He didn't. But he looked as though he might one day talk Death into switching service providers, and frankly, that was often enough. He belonged to every club that involved chairs and biscuits, captained nothing of consequence, and spoke with the economy of a man charged by the syllable. People mistook this for poise. It was, in fact, fatigue.

Together, they were not the stuff of ballads. They were the footnote you nearly skipped, until you realized it held the only truth in the chapter.

At Knox College, a place where intellect was prized, emotions were discouraged, and even the daffodils seemed to bloom apologetically, spring did not so much arrive as loiter. It slouched across the quad in muddy shoes and a suspicious coat, interrupting students' concentration with gusts of wind that smelled faintly of damp corduroy and crushed ambition.

It was during this petulant thaw, when everything and everyone seemed vaguely waterlogged, that the student council, drunk on a surplus budget and existential boredom, revived an old tradition long buried beneath good sense and several complaints to administration.

They called it Sadie Hawkins Day: an evening of mock weddings, reverse-proposals, and relationship cosplay performed in the spirit of feminist chaos and light-hearted regret.

The concept was charmingly grotesque: women would ask the men. The consequences, predictably, were unmitigated carnage.

Posters appeared overnight like a bad rash. *"Wed for a Night, Regret for a Lifetime!"* they chirped in fonts that suggested a unicorn had vomited optimism. Sign-up sheets bloomed in dormitory hallways, already cluttered with panicked roommate notices and "Lost: One Philosophy Textbook, Possibly Soul" flyers. A cardboard chapel was erected in the gymnasium by theatre majors who hadn't slept in 72 hours but were deeply committed to the emotional truth of hot glue and tulle.

And then there was Judy Gleason, who viewed romance the way others viewed unexplained foot rashes, with curiosity, irritation, and a vague hope that it would go away on its own.

She was halfway through *Thucydides* and on her third cup of tea that tasted vaguely like boiled wallpaper paste when Barbara Fowler appeared, sorority social chair, campus optimism peddler, and a girl who'd once described Tolstoy as "a bit of a downer."

Barbara wasn't exactly a friend, more a cheerful classroom presence who hadn't yet clocked that Judy's polite nods weren't an invitation to linger. But social cues were not Barbara's strong suit. She spoke to everyone as if they'd just agreed to be bridesmaids in her future wedding.

And so, with the inevitability of a sitcom plot twist, Barbara landed in the seat opposite Judy like a particularly determined parrot. Her clipboard hit the table with a satisfying smack.

"You simply must pick someone, Judy," she gushed, as though this were a rescue mission and Judy was the last kitten in the tree. "The deadline is tonight, and we need even numbers. And you… you are tragically unwed."

"An excellent observation," Judy said flatly, not looking up from her book. "Would you like to catalogue my tax records while you're at it?"

Barbara leaned in, eyes aglow with matchmaking derangement. "Jim Valentine," she whispered, as if revealing state secrets. "Tall. Stoic. Remarkably symmetrical. He'd look smashing in mock-tweed.

A classic groom."

Judy sighed. "Barbara, he once referred to Franz Kafka as 'the guy who hated furniture.'"

"Exactly! He's harmless. Reliable. He has the emotional temperature of wet toast. That's what you want in a fake husband. Low risk. Low drama."

Judy gave her a long, withering look. "I once translated Cicero's *De Officiis* in the original Latin because I found dating too intellectually humiliating. And you want me to wed the human equivalent of a comfortable armchair?"

Barbara simply smiled. "You'll thank me when you're posing under fairy lights with a paper ring and mild embarrassment."

"We'll see about that."

***

Jim was, as expected, in the reference section of the library, surrounded by old parliamentary records and the scent of disuse. He sat cross-legged on the carpet, as though he'd been there since the invention of ink, and was halfway through a paper on Victorian tax law that no one, not even Queen Victoria, had ever cared about.

Judy stood above him like divine judgment in loafers.

"Valentine," she said, not bothering to sit. "Stand up. You're being conscripted."

Jim looked up slowly, the way a tortoise might consider an oncoming bicycle. "Am I being arrested?"

"Worse. I'm proposing."

There was a silence in which you could hear the library's one functional radiator sigh in despair.

Jim closed his book and leaned back against the shelf with the resigned air of a man who had just remembered he left the oven on in 1982. "Is this one of those dreams where I forgot my trousers and I'm back in Catholic school?"

"No," Judy replied. "It's the Sadie Hawkins Day."

"Oh, that." He scratched his chin. "I thought it was a marketing stunt for the new dining hall sandwiches."

"Sadly, no. It's a campus-wide theatre of collective humiliation. I'm expected to participate."

He blinked. "And you chose me. That seems… off-brand."

"You're six feet four and statistically unlikely to start a flash mob," she replied. "Barbara Fowler assured me you 'clean up well' and own shoes that aren't sneakers."

"I do," he said. "I just can't remember where I put them. Somewhere under my sense of self-worth, I expect."

Judy extended the clipboard. "Sign this, and I'll stop talking."

He took it, read the title, *MOCK MARRIAGE CONSENT FORM (nonbinding in all countries)* and signed it without hesitation.

"You didn't even read the waiver," Judy noted.

"I trust you," he said, handing it back. "Which is probably a mistake. But you speak in declarative sentences, and I find that strangely soothing."

Judy blinked. "You are alarmingly easy to wed."

Jim stood and dusted off his trousers. "And you are alarmingly persuasive."

They stared at each other, each faintly amused, faintly bewildered, and both wondering why this suddenly felt like the most serious nonsense either of them had ever committed to.

"Well," Jim said at last, stretching. "Should I prepare a speech? Vows? A backup plan in case someone brings glitter?"

"No vows," Judy said. "This isn't *King Lear*. Just wear something less tragic than usual. And don't be late."

He nodded. "Wouldn't dream of it, my darling paper bride."

She rolled her eyes and walked off.

Behind her, Jim reopened his book, though he didn't read it. He sat quietly for a moment, staring at the corner of the page and wondering, with a strange flutter of foreboding delight, what on earth he'd just agreed to.

***

That Saturday, the gymnasium, already an architectural offence punishable by aesthetic law, had been redecorated to resemble a wedding chapel as envisioned by a group of highly motivated, terminally sleep-deprived theatre majors with a fondness for glitter and a loose grip on reality.

Silk flowers, possibly from a clearance bin marked *Funeral Extras*, drooped mournfully from the basketball hoops. Someone had rigged a tinny speaker to loop Wagner's *Bridal Chorus*, although it sounded more like the funeral march of a small, haunted music box.

A banner hung precariously over the chaos, proudly declaring:

"Lasso Yourself a Man, Happy Sadie Hawkins Day!"

…complete with a lopsided horseshoe graphic and a font that looked personally offended by its assignment.

Couples queued with the solemnity of lambs at a particularly ironic abattoir. They stood beneath strings of plastic ivy and fairy lights that flickered with the same nervous energy as the chaperones. At the center of it all, framed by an altar constructed from rusting chemistry lab stools and one visibly traumatized cello case, stood Leonard Bixby, philosophy major, self-declared existential priest, and man who wore his mother's choir robe with all the pomp of a bishop in exile.

He held a clipboard, a glitter-studded Bible (abridged), and a gavel someone had mistaken for a ceremonial bell. His expression suggested he was either about to perform a wedding or issue a parking fine.

Judy Gleason arrived not with grace but with purpose. She wore a green velvet dress that looked suspiciously like it had once hung in the drapery department of a defunct stately home. It did not swish. It *commanded*. Her hair was pinned like a fortress wall. Her expression implied she had already filed a complaint with the gods.

Jim followed at a safe distance, clad in what might generously be described as formalwear, or, more accurately, a wool suit that defied tailoring, seasonal relevance, and probably several fire codes. A pink carnation had been stabbed into his lapel at an angle that could only be described as *hopeful*. He looked like a man who had accidentally wandered into a school play and decided, against his better instincts, to stay.

They stood in line behind a girl dressed as Marie Antoinette and ahead of two juniors in a novelty horse costume. Front half was drunk. Back half had clearly lost a bet.

When their names were finally bellowed across the gym floor like lottery numbers, Judy stepped forward with the serene inevitability of someone walking into a controlled demolition.

Leonard cleared his throat like an amateur opera singer warming up.

"Do you, Judith Eleanor Gleason, take this man to be your lawfully pretend-husband, in overcooked pasta and undercooked ambition, through awkward group projects and fluorescent lighting, until the clock strikes twelve and sanity returns?"

Judy did not blink. "I suppose."

Leonard turned with a theatrical flourish. "And do you, James Arthur Valentine, take this formidable woman as your academic spouse, to honor, to begrudgingly admire, and to fear slightly during exams, for the duration of this performance art piece masquerading as a tradition?" Jim paused. "Only if she agrees not to quiz me on Roman tax codes over dessert."

There was polite laughter. Or perhaps someone sneezed.

A ring was produced, lavender construction paper, held together by Scotch tape and the collective will of the delusional. Judy slid it onto Jim's finger with the grave precision of a monarch knighting a particularly disappointing subject.

Flashbulbs popped. Someone whistled. A distant scream suggested the punch had finally been spiked. Near the bleachers, a freshman lost consciousness beside the piñata meant to resemble Cupid.

Jim looked down at the ring. "This feels… vaguely actionable."

"That's because it probably is," Judy murmured, adjusting his boutonnière like she was disarming a bomb. "Smile for the camera. You're now half-married and fully absurd."

They stood side by side beneath the flickering lights, surrounded by confetti shaped like birds that no longer flew and the sound of simulated joy. Couples swayed beneath a disco ball shaped, for some reason, like a Rubik's Cube. Someone in the background shouted, "Kiss her!" and someone else tripped over a tuba.

Judy surveyed the scene with the clinical detachment of a war correspondent.

Jim merely stood there, bemused, sparkling faintly, and increasingly aware that something very strange had just occurred.

In that brief moment, beneath the borrowed robe, the crooked banner, and the smell of cheap carnations and impending adulthood, something stirred. Not love, certainly not. That would've been wildly premature and against character. But something quieter. A flicker of intrigue. The vague, unsettling sense that the universe had just scribbled a footnote on their lives and titled it: Pay attention.

Jim tucked the fake marriage certificate into his inner jacket pocket.

Just in case.

***

After the matrimonial spectacle and a brief existential reckoning with their paper vows, Jim and Judy made a pilgrimage, as was customary among the newly faux-wed, to the most sacred site of student release: *Cherry Street.*

The Cherry Street was a pub only in the sense that it served liquids and dimmed the lights after 6 p.m. It had once been a carpet warehouse, judging by the smell, and still featured a mysterious back room no one entered except to come out slightly changed. The walls were lined with mismatched portraits of mustachioed Victorians, none labelled, all judging. A jukebox hummed softly in the corner, usually playing a song half a beat behind your mood.

It was the kind of place where the chairs wobbled, and the lighting made everyone look mildly haunted. The air smelled faintly of spilt beer and unresolved father issues. Behind the bar stood a man known only as Cliff, whose primary qualifications included a moustache of mythic proportions and the uncanny ability to pour drinks without ever making eye contact.

Jim slid onto a cracked vinyl stool. Judy didn't sit so much as *arrange herself*, as if posing for a Renaissance portrait.

Jim tapped a quarter on the bar. "One beer, please. The usual flavorless tragedy."

Cliff nodded silently and poured something amber and vaguely legal into a glass that looked like it had survived several wars.

Judy perused the cocktail list, a battered little booklet offering such dubious inventions as "The Giggle Water Special" and something called "The Red Menace," which seemed both politically and medically inadvisable.

She lifted a brow. "Tell me, Jim. Do you think ordering a Manhattan here counts as irony or a cry for help?"

Jim tilted his glass toward her. "Can't it be both?"

"I admire your optimism." She turned to Cliff. "A Manhattan. Make it strong enough to erase the last forty-five minutes of my life."

Cliff didn't speak. He simply nodded once, slowly, as if accepting a curse, and set to work.

Jim leaned on the bar. "You know that drink costs three times more than mine."

"Yes," Judy said, crossing her legs like a woman preparing to cross-examine. "That's because it's made with ingredients not found in old dental offices."

"Fair," Jim conceded. "But my beer didn't come with emotional baggage."

Judy accepted her cocktail, garnished with a lone cherry that looked exhausted. She took a sip, blinked once, and said, "Well. That'll do."

"Why a Manhattan?" Jim asked, already halfway through his beer. "It's loud. Complicated. Overdressed. Kind of like a cocktail party with opinions."

"I find it... aspirational," she said. "Besides, it looks like something Katharine Hepburn would drink while judging people."

"Which is, I assume, your preferred state of being."

"Obviously."

They drank in companionable silence for a moment as the jukebox played something mournful and off-key. A couple nearby was arguing over the difference between Freud and Jung. Cliff was gently swatting a raccoon away from the kitchen door with a bar towel.

Jim glanced sideways. "So. When you fake-proposed to me earlier..."

"Mm?"

"…did you choose me because I looked reliable, or because everyone else had already been claimed by other girls?"

Judy swirled her drink thoughtfully. "Neither. Barbara Fowler told me you 'clean up well.' I thought that sounded like an intriguing challenge."

"You make romance sound like a home renovation show."

"Well," she said, "you do have the energy of a man trying to fix his own radiator without reading the manual."

He laughed, in spite of himself. "That's the nicest thing anyone's ever said to me over 25-cent beer."

She raised her glass. "To doomed marriages and economically sound alcohol."

"To unlikely grooms and suspicious cherries."

They clinked. The cherry in her glass bobbed mournfully, like it knew it didn't belong here.

By the time Judy finished her second Manhattan and Jim had written his second $2 check with increasingly uncertain handwriting, they were both pleasantly flushed and leaning slightly toward each other, conspiratorial, amused, just a little bewildered by how not-terrible the evening had turned out. "Are you drunk?" she asked, watching him sign another check with a flourish that would've made a 19th-century gentleman proud.

"No," Jim said, then paused. "But I am experiencing financial vertigo."

She smirked. "You know you're not impressing me, right?"

"I'm not trying to impress you," he said. "I'm just trying to survive you."

She raised a brow. "How's that going?"

"I'll let you know when I'm no longer buying drinks with promissory notes."

****

The night peaked, as all good nights do, beneath the flickering gasps of Williston Hall dormitory lights and the looming specter of curfew, a grim 10 p.m. enforced by a trio of campus matrons in trench coats, orthopedic shoes, and disapproval sculpted into a weaponized form.

Judy, dressed like a duchess fallen on interesting times, took one look at the staircase ahead and declared it negotiable.

She placed a high heel on the bottom step.

The other foot, however, issued a formal notice of retirement and crumpled like a wilted marionette.

Jim caught her with the reflexes of a man who'd had just enough alcohol to believe in heroism but not enough to be good at it.

"Right," he muttered, steadying her by the elbow. "One floor. Seventeen steps. Mild incline. Easy."

He proceeded to escort Judy up the staircase one creak at a time, with the reverence of someone balancing a cake they didn't bake and definitely couldn't replace. She laughed musically, distantly, perhaps at him. Her perfume smelled of something French and judgmental. The stairs smelled like linoleum and panic.

"Don't look down," she murmured.

"I'm not," he grunted. "I'm looking *up*…at my doomed future, probably."

They reached the landing after an ascent worthy of Everest, albeit with fewer sherpas and more perfume. Judy paused at her door, one hand braced on the frame like a shipwrecked queen.

Jim exhaled with the weight of a man who had spent 75 cents on someone else's drink and 15 minutes climbing a stairwell with a passenger.

'I am probably not dating…ever again. Never ever,' he kept repeating to himself silently, with the solemnity of a man reliving wartime.

The financial hemorrhage. The drink selection. The stair-lift cosplay.

"It was," he thought, "a bit much."

But of course, he did.

Because logic is no match for affection wrapped in absurdity. And sometimes, the people you're quite certain you won't marry are the ones you end up carrying up staircases, buying overpriced cocktails for, and growing old beside, still slightly out of breath.

And that, he would admit decades later, was the most expensive 75 cents he ever spent.

And the best.

II

It had been seven months since Jim graduated. In that time, the world had lurched forward without asking for permission. Knox had ushered in another class of students who still believed finals could be aced with last-minute cramming and good posture. Jim had graduated with little ceremony and a certificate that looked oddly water-damaged despite perfect weather. Judy, meanwhile, was still deep in academia, orbiting around her political theory courses and eyeing secondary teaching applications like they might personally offend her.

Winter had descended on Chicago like a debt collector: grey, insistent, and immune to charm. Sidewalks glittered with salt. Shop windows displayed tinseled optimism. And Union Station, that grand old dame of rail travel, puffed and groaned under the weight of holiday traffic and too many wool coats.

Judy arrived with the sort of calm competence reserved for women who knew exactly which train car to board and refused to acknowledge delays as anything other than personal slights. She wore a green wool coat belted tightly at the waist and carried a bag that could have sustained a small expedition. The moment she stepped onto the platform, she was enveloped by the sort of industrial chill that made you question your blood's commitment to circulation.

Jim had spent that Friday in training at the Union Special factory in Huntley, Illinois. Afterward, he had just enough time to make the 55-mile drive downtown to Chicago's Loop to meet the Burlington Zephyr, arriving from Galesburg and points west. Fortunately, he had his little TR3, which made navigating the city easier. First, he double-parked on Wabash to pick up the engagement ring, bought with his freshly received Christmas bonus, then hurried west across the Loop to Union Station.

Earlier that December, his father had casually asked, "Why don't you give Judy a ring?"

Jim's typically vague reply: "I just talked to her."

Jim entered the station at the top of the grand staircase and spotted Judy just exiting the track gate where the train pulled in. He was holding a modest bouquet of carnations and looking like a man who had considered three other options before deciding flowers were both safe and unlikely to backfire.

"You're early," Judy said, stepping close.

"You're predictable," he replied. "It's endearing."

"You mean efficient."

He offered the bouquet. "Happy Christmas."

She took them with a slight smirk. "I hope you didn't steal these from a grave."

"Only emotionally."

The Drake Hotel, for those unfamiliar, was the sort of place where the carpets swallowed your footsteps and the chandeliers judged your posture. Their destination: the Camellia Room, known for its white tablecloths, crystal glasses, and clientele who knew better than to pronounce the "t" in filet.

Jim had booked the table three weeks in advance, a feat of planning that shocked even himself. The maître d', upon seeing their reservation, gave a small nod that suggested approval or mild gastrointestinal distress; it was difficult to say.

They were seated in a plush banquette, wedged together in the polite intimacy of upscale dining. A waiter in a waistcoat so crisp it could've sliced bread appeared with menus and an eyebrow raised in practiced anticipation.

Jim ordered a steak. Judy ordered trout. They agreed on wine, which came in a bottle that cost more than Jim's entire monthly grocery bill. The Camellia Room did not cater to frugality.

As the bread arrived, three small rolls arranged with military precision, Jim leaned over and said, in his most innocent tone, "You should call your mother. Let her know you arrived in one piece."

Judy raised an eyebrow. "She assumes that unless notified otherwise."

"Still. Use the table phone. It's very… modern."

Indeed, a rotary telephone had been wheeled over on its own small table, like a guest with a title. Judy picked up the receiver and dialed with casual grace.

Jim looked for the ring box in his inner coat pocket, which was naturally, right next to a crumpled bus ticket and a worn peppermint. He quickly realized he had forgotten to take it out of his overcoat pocket and left to retrieve it from the coat check, and made his way back to the table.

Judy was still on the phone.

"Yes, Mother… no, the train was on time… yes, he met me at the station… carnations, actually… no, not funeral flowers, just red ones…"

Jim slid back into the booth, nodded at the waiter, who was watching the scene with the unblinking attention of a man who'd seen several proposals and at least one incident involving a soufflé and tears, and waited for his moment.

As Judy was talking, Jim popped the velvet box open and slid it toward her like a man offering not just a ring but the resolution to a very long sentence.

She stared at it. Then at him.

There was a pause, long enough to fit an entire string quartet and possibly a gospel choir.

"You're proposing," she said finally.

"I'm hoping," he replied.

She looked back down at the ring. Modest, elegant, not so large as to scream insecurity but shiny enough to indicate intent. "Where was the speech?" she asked, dry as ever.

"In my coat. Next to the chewing gum."

"Of course."

She picked up the ring and examined it with the eye of someone who knew diamonds were not investments but obligations. And then, with a small, barely visible shrug, she slid it onto her finger.

"I assume this means yes?" he ventured.

She nodded. "Unless you've just given me an heirloom to hold while you flee the country."

"No such luck."

Judy then said to her mother we're engaged. I'll see you later and hung up.

Their food arrived precisely then, trout garnished with something delicate and green, steak bleeding politely into the plate. No one clapped. No one swooned. Just a quiet table with two people moving forward, side by side, as if they'd always known it would come to this.

Judy took a sip of wine. "I'll need to phone my mother again."

"Wait until dessert," Jim said. "Give her time to recover."

"From what?"

"From you marrying me."

She raised her glass.
"To tolerating each
other." "To quietly
surprising one
another," he returned.

And there it was.

No orchestra. No tears. Just two souls who didn't require spectacle to make meaning. She didn't need a kneel. He didn't need a script. And neither of them needed proof beyond the moment and the quiet weight of a ring.

It wasn't cinematic. But it was perfectly them.

Awkward. Honest. And unexpectedly lovely.

III

By the spring of 1962, Jim had just about begun to pretend he was a civilian. With his job hired right out of Knox at Union Special, where industrial sewing machines were built with the kind of grit usually reserved for coal miners and mothers of four. He was even looking at mortgage rates, granted, mostly in the newspaper margins while doodling tanks and question marks, but still, it was a gesture toward adulthood.

Judy was back at Knox, sending letters that smelled faintly of library glue and sensible perfume, occasionally enclosing clippings from *Ladies' Home Journal* with handwritten notes like, *"Page 32. We're not having those curtains."*

And then the Army, punctual as ever when ruining perfectly good plans, came calling.

As an ROTC graduate, Jim had always known it might happen. He just hadn't expected it to happen quite so soon, or with such complete indifference to the September wedding he and Judy had penciled in on the family calendar with light optimism and a dull pencil.

He received his orders while still sweating through drills at Aberdeen Proving Ground in Maryland, a base famous for its mud, mosquitoes, and men losing the will to live during mess inspections. Deployment: Germany. No negotiation. No delay.

Jim made the call in a booth near the barracks, where the phone still required the exact right amount of coinage and prayer.

"Well," he said, attempting casual bravery, "we can get married now, or we wait a couple of years."

A pause. Long enough for him to start rehearsing an apology.

"All right," Judy said, crisply. "We'll do it now."

And just like that, Operation Matrimony began, with the same urgency as a kitchen fire and roughly the same emotional delicacy.

Judy and her mother had exactly four weeks to plan a proper church wedding. Not the casual hypothetical one from earlier in the year, but a real affair with tulle, relatives, and arguments about ham.

They hit the ground running.

Veil shopping took place in a downtown department store whose bridal consultant had the charm of a malfunctioning vending machine and the taste of a defrosted grapefruit. Judy tried on five gowns before settling on one that didn't make her look like she was about to greet guests at the coronation of Queen Elizabeth. Her mother declared it "dignified," which was the highest compliment available for a wedding dress.

Meanwhile, Jim was in Maryland learning how to polish his boots until he could see his reflection, and question his life choices in it. He spent his days crawling through obstacle courses and folding socks like he owed them an apology.

Wedding planning updates arrived via telegram, postcard, and once, through a very long-distance phone call patched through an operator who sniffed disapprovingly whenever Judy said the word "honeymoon."

Back in Illinois, the pre-wedding chaos reached full pitch.

At the Gleason house, the dining room became a war room of stationery, place cards, and frosting trials. There was a heated debate over whether the cake should be chocolate or vanilla until someone pointed out that Jim wouldn't notice either way.

Uncle Harold demanded to bring his accordion. Cousin Maureen announced she would arrive with a date "from the bowling alley," prompting Judy's father to suggest separate seating arrangements. Judy's mother drew a new chart in red pencil with the kind of precision usually reserved for military campaigns.

The week before the wedding, Judy sat on the back porch, still in curlers, eating a sandwich that had once resembled tuna.

Jim, home on leave Thursday night for exactly seven days, including Saturday, sat beside her. He wore his Army-issue-trousers and a jacket that looked like it had lost a fight with a steam press.

"This feels surreal," he said.

"You look surreal," she replied. "Did they measure your sleeves properly, or just eyeball it and hope for the best?"

He grinned. "They asked my opinion and went from there."

Judy handed him a lemon bar wrapped in wax paper. "Eat something before my mother makes you test cake frosting again. We've gone through four kinds. My aunt says you're too thin."

"Your aunt thinks Bing Crosby is too thin."

"She's consistent."

The porch swing creaked beneath them.

"Are we really doing this?" he asked.

"We are," she said, wiping powdered sugar from his collar.

"You know, we could have eloped."

She gave him a sidelong glance. "And deny my grandmother the chance to judge every boutonnière? Absolutely not."

They sat in companionable silence as a neighbor's radio floated over the yard, *Perry Como* warbling something vaguely romantic, the kind of song you slow-danced to while hoping your tie wasn't crooked.

The ceremony itself was brisk, lovely, and slightly damp, Chicago weather refusing to cooperate with propriety. The church was full of friends, family, and one suspiciously loud umbrella that refused to stay shut.

Jim wore a rented morning suit Friday after arriving Thursday night, that fit him like a borrowed opinion. Judy walked down the aisle with Bill, her father, in that dignified dress, holding a bouquet of lilies furnished by cousin Micky McGuire, along with all the church and reception flowers. There was no dramatic pause. No sweeping declarations. Just a soft "I do," and a matching one in reply.

The reception took place. The gifts were modest, some monogrammed towels, a percolator, a set of Pyrex bowls that would last longer than several presidents. Four-day honeymoon.

Judy would join Jim in Germany in a week once the paperwork cleared and she convinced the airline she could, in fact, survive on half a suitcase and a prayer.

They parted at the train station two days later. He in uniform. She in a sensible coat with a hopeful smile and red lipstick that didn't smudge when she kissed him goodbye.

"You'll write?" she asked.

"Like a man with nothing better to do," he said.

And then he was gone.

Just like that. No orchestra. No slow fade to black.

Just two people, married now. Not for show. Not for spectacle.

But because it was the thing to do. And somehow, in all its wartime logic and scrambled execution, it was precisely what they wanted.

Chapter 2

Shortly after their honeymoon, barely enough time to wash the mosquito bites and pine sap from their clothes, Jim was off. The U.S. Army, with its famously romantic sense of timing, summoned him to Nellingen, Germany. Judy, armed with little more than a suitcase, a new surname, and a wedding ring that sparkled modestly in the sunlight, would follow him soon after.

The flight itself was an experience. Judy, ever the portrait of poise, found herself wedged between a coughing Bavarian tourist and a nun with strong elbows and a firm view on armrest ownership. The engine roared like it was offended by the sky, the coffee tasted faintly of regret, and the stewardess wore a smile as fixed as the emergency oxygen masks.

When the plane finally touched down in Frankfurt, Judy stepped out like a debutante arriving at a debut she hadn't rehearsed for. Her heels clicked on the tarmac with a kind of American determination. The air smelled like damp stone and bureaucracy. Somewhere nearby, a man barked at a dog, and the dog barked back in German.

Jim met her at the arrivals gate, looking like a man caught between military discipline and romantic obligation. His uniform was pressed, his shoes shined, and in his hand, a slightly wilted bouquet of daisies wrapped in what appeared to be butcher paper.

"They didn't have proper wrapping," he said by way of introduction.

Judy eyed the flowers. "Well, I suppose meat-grade daisies are better than none."

He offered them like a man handing over evidence. "They were the last bouquet not involving glitter."

She accepted them with grace and just a touch of theatrical suffering. "You spoil me."

"It was either this or an ashtray shaped like a castle. Frankfurt's finest."

After living in the BOQ (bachelor-officer-quarters) for a week, they found a GI from the post who spoke German and was familiar with the needs of new soldiers accompanied by their wives. He was able to get us a used Opel and direct us to a dwelling that was for rent. The drive to their new home took them past rows of barbed wire fences, onion-domed churches, and a cow who, judging by its expression, had seen some things. Their flat was in the basement of a gray-stoned building that looked like it had survived the war simply out of spite.

Inside, it was furnished in what Jim referred to as "G.I. Gothic." That is: metal beds, one chest of drawers, and a kettle that whistled like it was mourning the Queen. The windows stuck in winter and the toilet groaned like a guilty conscience.

Still, Judy surveyed the space and declared, "All right, we'll make it look less like a cell block."

"How?" Jim asked.

"Curtains," she replied with the confidence of a woman who had once tamed wedding chaos with a single hairpin.

The first week was spent negotiating with appliances. The oven had two settings: off and on, the stovetop demanded flattery, and the plumbing offered commentary on the hour. Judy developed a friendship with a neighbor named Evelyn, a fellow Army wife who had two toddlers, and the voice of someone who didn't believe in warm welcomes but offered a cup of chicory coffee anyway.

"She's nice," Jim observed after meeting Evelyn.

"She offered me a potato and a curse word," Judy said. "I like her."

Meanwhile, Jim was dispatched daily to the base where he worked in an ordinance company that repaired tanks and small arms.

"You know what they served at lunch in the mess today?" Jim asked one evening, unlacing his boots with the weariness of someone who had marched in circles for democracy.

"Tell me," Judy said, folding laundry with the resigned elegance of royalty in exile.

"Something called 'Victory Hash.' I believe it was losing."

She tossed a sock at his head. "You married into this."

"Yes, but I didn't realize it came with diplomatic immunity to seasoning."

They made friends. Slowly. Quietly. Mostly with other couples who also had no furniture and a suspicious amount of canned peaches. Dinners were potluck affairs where everyone brought what they had, which was usually Spam and optimism. Judy became known for her ability to stretch a single onion across four meals and a diplomatic incident.

They learned to ride bikes along cobbled paths, to point at pastries instead of pronouncing them, and to say "danke" with just the right level of gratitude and defeat.

Sundays were spent walking through villages where the churches chimed every fifteen minutes like an overenthusiastic grandmother, and old men played chess outside bakeries, pausing only to squint at Americans with the benevolent suspicion usually reserved for raccoons near bins.

One rainy afternoon, they took a day trip to Heidelberg, sharing a picnic on the riverbank under a collapsed umbrella.

"Do you think we'll ever own a sofa?" Jim asked, chewing on a sandwich that may have once been ham.

"Eventually," Judy replied.

He nodded solemnly. "We'll cover it in a nice throw."

"Of course. Something cheerful. Like black."

In time, their tiny quarters became less gray and more *theirs*. Judy tacked up a photograph of Lake Michigan. Jim added a dented tin where they collected loose change and foreign coins. A record player arrived via a very dubious postal route, and soon their evenings filled with jazz, static, and the occasional knock from a neighbor asking if they could please keep it down, some of us are trying to remember what America sounded like before Elvis.

And through it all, showers in the kitchen, water heaters on the wall, army drills, and beer stronger than local opinions, Judy and Jim built something stronger than furniture.

They built routine. And laughter. And the quiet comfort of two people who didn't need grand things, just real ones.

Because back then, love didn't need a chandelier. It just needed good shoes, a working kettle, and someone who knew how to reheat potatoes without losing their will to live.

And Judy, for the record, had mastered all three.

***

Their landlords, Eric and Ruth Schweitzer, lived directly above them. Eric, an executive at Mercedes-Benz, wore crisp shirts and the expression of someone who had once stared down both war and underperforming employees. As it turned out, he had been a tank driver during the war in Holland. Later, he was transferred to the Russian front, which was a move he described with the enthusiasm of someone recalling a failed root canal. Captured by the Russians, he spent four post-war years as a POW before returning home with a deep hatred for Communism and a profound appreciation for anyone bearing peanut butter and American cigarettes.

He liked Jim immediately.

Eric and Ruth became fast friends. The monthly rent ritual began with formalities that would make a banker blush. Judy and Jim, armed with their $67 housing allowance from the Army, would ascend the stairs and hand over the exact amount, never a mark more or less. The transaction always included small talk, Ruth's almond biscuits, and at least one heavily nostalgic story from Eric's tank-driving days.

Over time, the financial arrangement gained flavor. Eric discovered that American post exchanges contained a wealth of treasures utterly absent from German shelves. Lawn mowers, for instance. At the time, he was mowing his lawn with a scythe and a stare of pure determination. When he spotted the Black & Decker electric mower Jim had casually mentioned in conversation, his eyes lit up like a man who'd seen God. The barter was swift: one lawn mower, one month's rent. Deal.

From there, the exchanges continued: peanut butter for replacement parts, shaving cream for window cleaner, and once, a pack of Oreos in exchange for borrowing Eric's vacuum cleaner, which sounded like a jet engine and may have actually had a jet engine inside.

Years later, Eric and Ruth visited Jim and Judy in the United States. They brought chocolates, photos, and Ruth's steely insistence that American dish soap was far too gentle. The friendship endured, even as the basement apartment faded into memory.

Still, whenever Jim and Judy thought back to their early days in Germany, they didn't just remember the apartment or the strange laundry pot or the electric shower that judged them from above. They remembered the people. The barter deals. The rituals. And the absurd, unexpected joy of starting a life in a place where even the simplest things, like doing laundry, felt like a quest from a German fairytale.

***

The rain tapped against the window of their modest flat like a nosy neighbor who knew too much. Jim, freshly pressed in his second lieutenant uniform, squinted at the crossword puzzle on the kitchen table. Judy emerged from the bathroom, towel over her shoulder, eyes wide.

"Jim," she said.

He didn't look up. "Fifteen across. Four letters. Starts with 'B'... synonym for disaster."

"Jim," she said again, sharper.

He looked up this time. "What is it? Did we run out of coffee again?"

She handed him a white stick with a pink plus sign.

He blinked. Then again.

"Well. That's not a thermometer."

Judy exhaled, somewhere between a laugh and a sigh. "We're pregnant."

He sank into the chair, staring at nothing. "We just figured out the washing machine." A beat. "And now... a baby?" He rubbed his temples. "We skipped a few steps, Judy."

"Surprise!" she said, arms outstretched like a ta-da.

He stood and hugged her tightly. "Well, hell. Let's make this the best accidental planning we ever didn't do."

Somehow, it all felt like the beginning of something.

Pregnancy in Germany was not something Judy had planned. Then again, most of this wasn't planned. Getting married, moving to a country where she knew exactly four words, one of which was "schnitzel", and then finding out she was going to give birth in a place where nurses wore hats taller than their actual heads. But then came the glimmer: the U.S. military was footing the bill for all the medical care. And as fate, or small

Midwestern liberal arts colleges, would have it, the on-base doctor was a fellow Knox College alum.

Dr. Eugene Graham. TKE. Married to a Tri Delt. The kind of man who still called women "young lady" and meant it like it was 1956.

The first time Judy met him, she blinked at his name badge and deadpanned, "Small world."

Dr. Graham smiled politely. "Even smaller womb."

Jim tried not to laugh, but he failed, loudly.

From then on, every prenatal appointment was scheduled according to Dr. Graham's shifts. None of this roulette with whichever doctor happened to be around. No.

Judy had Knox privilege. It was like having a backstage pass to the gestational concert of her life.

"You're lucky," said another expectant mother in the waiting room, eyeing Judy's folder with envy. "I get Dr. Schnitt every time."

"Dr. Schnitt?" Judy whispered, horrified. "That sounds like a threat."

"It is."

***

Judy's parents, June and Bill, were ecstatic and made elaborate plans to cross the Atlantic, which in 1963 meant twelve different forms, six sets of immunization cards, and a blessing from the Pope, or close enough, Judy's grandmother, or as Judy lovingly called her, "Mother the Magnificent" also insisted on coming.

But funds were tight, and the family made a strategic deployment.

"Dad goes first," Judy explained over a crackling phone line. "Then Mom and Grandma after the baby arrives to, quote, 'examine the results.'"

"Like you're baking a casserole," Jim mumbled.

"And they're bringing thermometers."

Bill, when he arrived, was put up in the bachelor officers' quarters, much to the alarm of the other young officers who weren't expecting a civilian with strong opinions about furniture polish and American jazz. Within days, he had befriended Colonel Rayel, a man with a fondness for ironed uniforms, punctuality, and tequila. He was also, as it turned out, Mexican-American and carried with him the culinary vengeance of generations.

"You like spicy food?" the Colonel asked Bill over breakfast one morning.

"Love it," Bill declared, with a bravado he would later regret.

The Colonel raised one eyebrow and grinned. "We'll see."

What followed was a daily breakfast duel of escalating heat: green chiles, red chiles, and one morning, a sauce that made Bill go momentarily blind in one eye.

"You okay?" Jim asked, as Bill reached for the milk with trembling hands.

"No regrets," he rasped. "Just… maybe… smaller bites."

But beyond the spice warfare, the Colonel grew fond of Bill, perhaps because he treated him like a real person and not a civilian interloper. Soon, Bill was a regular fixture at early-morning battalion formations, watching Jim salute and fumble his way through command life.

"I like your father-in-law," Colonel Rayel told Jim one morning. "He's got nerve."

Jim nodded. "He says it's Midwestern humility mixed with misplaced confidence."

"Same thing that got me promoted."

And just like that, Jim found himself appointed to battalion staff as the new supply officer, a step up, if you ignored the bureaucratic chaos, endless forms, and requisition drama that came with trying to order three working staplers and getting seventeen boxes of socks instead.

***

As Judy neared her due date in May, Dr. Graham proposed a plan.

"I'm on duty today and tomorrow," he said, peering over her chart like it was a crossword puzzle. "We could induce. That way, I'll be here when it happens."

"Sounds sensible," Judy said.

"Sounds thrifty," Jim added, lowering his voice. "If we get the timing right, we avoid paying for an extra hospital day. It's five bucks a night."

Judy gave him a look. "Are you budgeting my uterus?"

"I'm budgeting our lives."

Dr. Graham, unbothered by the exchange, signed the papers.

So labor was induced. And in true military fashion, everything went off… almost on time.

Jimmie made his debut on May 17th, at exactly 1:05 a.m., technically late enough to save them five bucks.

"Victory," Jim whispered as he held his son for the first time, the new fatherly pride settling somewhere between awe and total terror.

"His head is lumpy," Judy said, exhausted but clear-eyed.

"All babies are lumpy."

"But he's… our lumpy."

∗∗∗

The calls to the States began immediately. Because of the time difference, everyone back home got the news on May 16th. Which meant, accidentally, that Jimmie now had two birthdays.

"Two cakes a year," Jim said. "The American dream."

"Don't get greedy," Judy murmured from her hospital bed.

"And two birth certificates," he added. "American and German. Technically makes him eligible for German citizenship."

"So he can grow up and tell people he was born in Germany, raised on bratwurst and bureaucracy."

"Exactly."

The German hospital had strict policies: one day in, out by dawn the next. Judy was barely finished with her tea when the nurse appeared at the door.

"Aufstehen!" the woman barked. "Time to go."

Judy looked down at the blood on her shoes from walking to breakfast and raised an eyebrow. "Do I at least get a sticker?"

"No. But you get to leave."

Meanwhile, Jim scrambled to find flowers. He had no idea where Germans kept their romance supplies. After walking in circles through cobblestoned markets in Esslingen, he found a stall that looked promising.

"Ich möchte… blumen," he tried.

The vendor, used to clueless soldiers in stiff uniforms, pointed to a bunch of tulips. Jim, overwhelmed, bought enough flowers to cover a small parade float. Negotiating the price was not an option. The vendor gave him the posted rate, perhaps out of mercy, or amusement.

When he returned to the hospital, arms full of blooms, Judy burst out laughing.

"Are you opening a florist shop?"

"No," Jim said, panting. "I'm trying to say 'I love you' in twelve bouquets."

She smiled, eyes tired but bright. "It's working."

Back at their quarters, the three of them, new parents, new life, new version of normal, sat in the quiet that only comes with newborns and military-issued furniture.

Jim looked at his son, who was quietly gurgling in a bassinet.

"Well," he said, "we're officially adults now."

Judy blinked. "We've been adults."

"No, this is different. This one cries, and we can't give him back."

She reached for his hand. "We'll figure it out."

Jim nodded. "We've got Dr. Graham, a colonel godfather, and German efficiency on our side. What could possibly go wrong?"

As it turned out, many things. But for now, they had each other, a child who got two birthdays, and the vague smell of tulips.

It was a start.

Chapter 3

There are moments in life that arrive with trumpets and confetti. The birth of Jimmie was not one of them.

Instead, it came with fluorescent lighting, mild panic, and a nurse who kept calling Jim "Dad" like he had just been promoted against his will. Still, when Jimmie entered the world, all eight pounds of him, red-faced and furious, something unspoken cracked open between them.

Judy counted all his fingers and toes immediately, like someone inspecting a new appliance for missing parts. "Ten," she announced triumphantly, as if Jim might've accidentally passed on a recessive toe-deficiency gene. She looked exhausted and glowing in that uniquely postpartum way, equal parts goddess and hostage. "He's perfect," she added, her voice hoarse, eyes wide.

He really was.

There was joy, yes. Immense joy. Also fear. But mostly, responsibility. Capital R. The kind that sets up camp between your shoulder blades and starts paying rent in stress knots. Jim suddenly understood that they were no longer two people trying to make a marriage work in a foreign country with a faulty washing machine. They were three.

And three changes the math.

No more dashing out the door for a last-minute coffee date or spontaneous road trip. No more mutually agreed-upon negligence. They were a unit now, bound together by love, obligation, and a baby who seemed suspiciously alert for someone born ten minutes ago.

It was a new portal, to borrow from the Scout manual Jim never quite returned. One of those invisible doors life keeps shoving you through with no warning and even less instruction. And once you're inside, there's no going back. The rules from childhood, once laminated and posted on every Boy Scout bulletin board, suddenly became not just quaint but crucial: **Trust. Loyalty. Helpful. Friendly. Courteous. Kind. Obedient. Cheerful. Thrifty. Brave. Clean. Reverent.** Also: burp cloths, sterile thermometers, and a sleep schedule straight from a CIA black site.

He said it like a mantra while pacing their tiny living room, one sock on, burping cloth slung over his shoulder, and a half-drunk cup of coffee cooling on the windowsill. Judy, half-asleep on the couch with Jimmie curled against her chest, cracked one eye open. "You planning to raise a baby or summon a deity?"

Jim didn't know.

They looked at their son. Then at each other. Then at the empty chair where one might expect, say, a helpful grandmother or wise elder to appear. But no one came. Judy's mother and grandmother were across the ocean, and the new parents, let's be honest, had as much experience with babies as they did with fine German beer, i.e., they'd heard about them in theory.

Neither of them had siblings. Neither of them had practiced burping a doll or identifying the mysterious patches on baby skin that either meant "completely normal" or "call the Red Cross."

They were hopeless. Which is why they turned to the Knox's family doctor, Dr. Graham, who, to this day, deserves his own stained-glass window in the cathedral of new parenthood.

Dr. Graham was the kind of man whose mere presence made you breathe slower. He looked vaguely like a friendly detective from a British murder mystery: calm, unhurried, with a tweed aura even when not in tweed.

Judy, with Jimmie curled against her chest, asked the question out loud: "What if we mess him up?"

Dr. Graham folded his hands like a monk and gave the answer that should be etched on every maternity ward door:

"Everything you do is right."

Jim blinked.

He repeated it. Slower this time, in case the sleep deprivation had taken out their comprehension centers. "Everything. You. Do. Is. Right. You love him? You're already doing it right."

Judy nodded slowly, her throat tightening. Jim felt his jaw unclench for the first time in days. It was like being told that despite the manual not existing, they'd somehow already memorized it. Native ability and formal education were there. But really, it was the permission to stop worrying about perfection and start living inside the imperfection of parenting.

So that's what they did.

They weren't flawless. The coffee got cold. They once left the nursery door cracked open, hoping to hear him if he cried, but some nights, even a mother's ears missed a sound. They used a German teething toy that they later discovered was meant for dogs. But somehow, astonishingly, Jim and Judy got through it.

They operated like a little village, small but determined. Jim and Judy were no longer individuals with dreams and calendars. They were a team, a trio, a unit under siege from sleep regressions and existential dread, and they loved each other more fiercely because of it.

Jimmie didn't know any of that, of course. He just stared at them like a tiny general, issuing wordless commands in the form of cries and gurgles.

But Jim and Judy followed his lead. They figured it out. And every time they walked through one of life's strange, demanding portals, they carried the weight and wonder of that first one with them.

And a burp cloth. Always the burp cloth.

Their days fell into a rhythm, clumsy, sleep-deprived, and stitched together with trial, error, and the occasional diaper disaster, but a rhythm nonetheless. Just as the couple began to feel they had the hang of their new life as parents, reinforcements arrived. Not the quiet kind, either.

***

The day June and Ermina arrived in Germany, the household population doubled and the apartment lost all illusions of quiet.

For both women, it was their first time crossing an ocean. June's excitement manifested in a relentless clutching of her handbag and continuous breathless commentary on everything from plane food to foreign signage. Ermina, meanwhile, surveyed the Frankfurt airport with the composed disdain of someone who still believed motorcars were a passing phase and that Europe could use a good mopping.

Then came immigration.

Two gates. One read **CITIZEN**. The other, **FOREIGNER**. Ermina, born in 1898 and a citizen of what she still called *The Republic*, marched confidently toward the **CITIZEN** gate, ignoring June's tug on her coat sleeve.

"I'm no foreigner," she announced.

The German official, tired, kind-eyed, and clearly trained for this, gently intercepted her. With a calm smile, he redirected her to the correct line. "This way, ma'am. Unless you are German?"

She sniffed. "Well, I certainly don't *feel* foreign."

June mouthed a silent apology as she trailed after her mother. For the rest of her life, Ermina referred to the incident as "that nonsense at the airport" and spoke of it as though she'd been the victim of diplomatic slander.

When they finally arrived at the apartment, it was not quite what they'd expected.

Three rooms: a small kitchen with a suspiciously humming refrigerator, a living room with a couch of dubious color and age, and a bedroom just large enough to house a full bed, a bassinet, and regrets about how many boxes they'd brought. But Ermina's first issue was not with the cramped quarters.

It was the missing front door.

The "apartment" was, in fact, a sectioned-off part of a longer hallway: three rooms with doors, yes, but nothing sealing them off from the hallway itself. It gave the impression that anyone walking past might pop in for coffee or offer unsolicited parenting tips.

Upon meeting Eric, Ermina said, "You appear to have forgotten to finish the building."

Two days later, a carpenter showed up with lumber, tools, and the reluctant air of a man who'd lost a bet. A real front door was installed. It creaked when it closed, but it closed, and that was enough. Ermina approved, and the building, it seemed, dared not challenge her again.

Inside, life began to take shape. Judy was still adjusting to motherhood, her days governed by feedings, laundry, and trying to remember what sleep felt like. She'd taken to narrating her thoughts aloud just to feel like a functioning adult.

Jim, when not on duty, tried to make himself useful, which mostly involved looking at things and asking, "Do you want me to hold him?" in increasing levels of confidence.

Jimmie himself was unconcerned with their efforts. He howled on schedule, peed unpredictably, and slept like a saint, just never when anyone else did.

June arrived bearing salvation: baby clothes. Since Judy hadn't had a proper baby shower (apparently "transatlantic baby registries" were not a thing yet), the layette had been sparse. But June opened her suitcase like a magician revealing her final trick. Out came a steady stream of onesies, knitted sweaters, impossibly tiny socks, and a blue cap with a fuzzy pom-pom. Judy held it like it was the crown jewels.

"Wait until you see the quilt," June said. "Made from your old high school T-shirts."

Judy stared at her mother for a beat. "You were *saving* those?"

"Of course. That's what mothers do. We hoard sentimentality and call it planning."

Still, practical needs remained. The PX offered limited baby supplies, and Judy had given up hope of finding a crib. Then there was Sgt. Peters, Jim's platoon sergeant and low-key miracle worker. He had the keys to every storeroom and a network of favors that likely spanned NATO. One casual conversation later, and a crib appeared, along with a gently used mobile that played a haunting rendition of *Twinkle, Twinkle, Little Star* in German. It would become the family lullaby for months, equal parts soothing and mildly unsettling.

Evenings at home took on a new rhythm. June cooked casseroles that defied local ingredients, and Ermina, after a few days of watching Judy like a hawk, finally handed her back the reins of her own household. She took to knitting in the living room instead, occasionally muttering observations like, "This radiator has no soul," and "I don't trust any country where the butter comes in tubes."

Judy found herself laughing more. She wasn't quite sure when it had happened, maybe it was watching her stoic grandmother try to operate a European washing machine, or Jim's attempts to change a diaper with military precision, but joy returned in small, surprising bursts.

***

By the time Jimmie was six days old, he'd already logged more history than most American high schoolers could cram before a final. His first grand outing was a full-scale Baroque palace tour. Naturally.

Ludwigsburg Palace stood in pristine defiance of centuries' worth of wars, fires, and questionable wallpaper trends. It was the sort of place with chandeliers that mocked gravity and staircases that existed solely to remind people of their inferior shoes. And there were Jim and Judy, standing at the entrance with a baby bundled up like a loaf of bread at a royal picnic.

Locals stared. German mothers whispered, appalled, as the squalling newborn made his international debut before he could hold his own head. Apparently, six days old was not considered sightseeing age. But Jimmie, undeterred, gurgled something into the palace air that drew nods and soft laughter from the docents. Maybe he had a handle on the language already. None of them dared question it.

Once Jimmie had graced royal halls, the paperwork caught up with the pomp. A passport was needed, an American passport, of course. Dual citizenship was legal, sure. But pledging allegiance to two flags felt like the diplomatic equivalent of dating two people who both think it's exclusive. Judy's passport was updated with a new photo featuring her and Jimmie, looking like a Renaissance Madonna and Child with a touch of postnatal exhaustion. As for Jim, he had his dog tags and military ID: two pieces of metal and a laminated card that somehow gave him clearance to cross borders, lead soldiers, and now, apparently, fatherhood.

By September, the novelty of parenthood had started to settle in, just in time for an influx of nostalgia. Gervaise, Judy's childhood best friend and their wedding's Maid of Honor, arrived in Nellingen. She had come to be Jimmie's godmother, but her real superpower was making Judy laugh the way only someone who knew her pre-bills, pre-marriage, and pre-3 a.m. feedings could. Gervaise's arrival was met with German pastries, celebratory strolls, and the kind of laughter that shakes the baby out of a nap in the stroller.

Sightseeing was taken up a notch. They hit every photogenic spot in the region: castles, cathedrals, and bierhoffs with menus longer than a training manual. Gervaise was appropriately enchanted, especially with the beer. Even Jimmie seemed pleased, blinking in approval from his buggy like a tiny, well-traveled emperor.

One dinner stood out. Colonel Rayel, already slated to be the godfather, invited them to the Officers' Club for an evening that was more silverware than sentiment, but heartfelt nonetheless. Jimmie slept through most of it, an early sign that he would develop good taste in food but low tolerance for long speeches.

But the moment that truly sealed Gervaise's place in family lore came when she passed by the battalion dining facility. There, in a bold sans-serif font, hung a sign that simply read:

CONSOLIDATED MESS

She stopped, tilted her head, and said, "Now, calling a kitchen a 'mess' is brave. But calling it a *consolidated* mess? That's just admitting defeat."

The soldiers nearby didn't know whether to laugh or salute.

Her wit, paired with Judy's warmth and Jimmie's newly acquired habit of smiling at old men with medals, turned that season into something golden. Our little three-room, now-with-door apartment became a lively hub of memories, laughter, and baby supplies smuggled in with help from Sergeant Peters and the occasional PX miracle.

It was a season of unlikely comfort, a baroque palace here, a carpenter's visit there, and the deep relief of hearing a friend joke in your native tongue over a steaming plate of schnitzel.

And so, life marched on: through ornate gates, past government offices, into christenings, and out the doors of consolidated messes, one chapter, one scene, and one giggling baby at a time.

Chapter 4

July 14th, Bastille Day, had always been someone else's celebration until now. For Jim and Judy, it had grown a second identity: an anniversary. One full year of marriage, parenthood, foreign languages, and the daily tightrope walk that was life on an American army post in Germany. A celebration was in order, and where better to mark the occasion than Paris?

Judy, who had minored in French at college and could still conjugate irregular verbs under pressure, floated the idea. Jim, fresh off buying a modestly chic gray Volkswagen Beetle with the last of their savings, saw no reason to argue. After a brief family summit, including 10-month-old Jimmie (whose approval was issued via enthusiastic gurgling), the decision was unanimous.

Their home in Nellingen had become a compact kingdom of routines and careful diplomacy. Judy handled the kitchen, the language barriers, and the general tone of the household. Jim took on car maintenance, military protocol, and practical logistics. Jimmie ruled them both with a burp cloth in one hand and an unpredictable sleep schedule.

Gas and cigarettes on the European economy were outrageously priced: $2.50 a gallon and nearly a dollar a pack. But on the base? Twenty-five cents flat. Jim, who viewed financial strategy as a form of sport, took this as a personal challenge. They loaded the roof rack with two five-gallon jerry cans and enough diapers to stage a small coup. The baby buggy was lashed down next to the gas cans, a juxtaposition that worried exactly no one.

The night before departure, none of them could sleep, not even Jimmie, who had an uncanny knack for sensing change in the air. By 4 a.m., they were dressed, packed, caffeinated, and backing out of the driveway. The morning was cool, damp, and eerily quiet.

Judy leaned her head against the window. "We're young, broke, and completely unqualified to navigate a foreign capital. Perfect."

Jim grinned. "Let's go be Americans in Paris."

The Autobahn stretched ahead like a promise. They had no maps, only Judy's recollections from college and Jim's overconfidence. Fortunately, road signs in Europe were generous with arrows and vowels. After hours of humming along at a modest clip (Jim didn't trust the VW past 70 km/h), they crested a rise and saw it: the Eiffel Tower, rising like a steel exclamation mark.

"Look!" Judy pointed. "We're actually doing this."

Jimmie sneezed. They took it as a sign of agreement.

***

Paris was welcoming in a way only cities older than your country can be: smug in its survival, smugger in its elegance. The Champs-Élysées stretched out like a red carpet that didn't care who walked it, unimpressed by the lumbering American family inching through side streets in their battle-worn VW Beetle. The car smelled of powdered formula and desperation.

"There it is!" Judy nearly shouted, sitting in the passenger seat with a paper bag of sterilized baby bottles on her lap, a map wedged under her thigh, and one sockless foot propped against the dashboard. The bag tipped, a bottle rolled out, and bounced somewhere under the clutch pedal.

Jim yanked the wheel like he was taking a corner in Le Mans. The VW squealed its disapproval but obeyed. A U-turn executed with the smug grace of a circus dog. They almost hit a Vespa. The driver, entirely unbothered, lit a cigarette and gave them a thumbs up.

Moments later, they rolled to a stop in front of the Hotel Gallia, a grand, ornate structure with polished brass fixtures and a doorman who looked like he moonlighted as an extra in a war film.

The man approached, trenchcoat flapping in the breeze like a flag of refined disappointment. He opened the door with a practiced elegance. Two of Jimmie's diapers tumbled out and hit the cobblestones like surrender flags.

"Bienvenue," the doorman said, stepping over the mess with Parisian indifference. "May I help you with your… belongings?"

Jim pointed toward the car. "The baby buggy and the gas can, please have them checked into the baggage room. We'll only take the suitcases upstairs."

The doorman hesitated. "Monsieur, gasoline at eight dollars per gallon? It may not be here in the morning."

Jim nodded grimly. "That's why it's going inside." He carried the gas can like contraband, while the buggy was wheeled off with the luggage, both officially tagged and stashed for navigating Paris later.

The suite at the Hotel Gallia was grander than anything they had ever set foot in. Cream walls, golden moldings, a sitting room with heavy velvet furniture that looked allergic to joy. Two bedrooms. Possibly a third, though they weren't quite sure.

"There's a reservation note here," Judy said, squinting at the neatly typed French. "An extra room for 'l'enfant.'"

Jim glanced around. "Wait…they think the baby needs his own room?"

"Do they know how babies work?" she asked.

Jimmie sneezed in response. Then burped. Then farted. The acoustics in the suite made it sound like cannon fire.

June and Bill had booked the suite as a gift: lavish, generous, and entirely mismatched. The furniture looked nervous. Judy laid a changing mat across the chaise longue, and Jim kept apologizing to the paintings. They spent one night in the velvet-trimmed bed, the baby between them in a travel bassinet. They didn't sleep. At 2 a.m., Jim wandered into the extra room, Jimmie's alleged quarters, and opened the window. Paris glittered below, oblivious to the anxious Americans in its midst.

"We need a place where we're not afraid to exhale," Judy said, sometime around sunrise, holding Jimmie close as she sat in an armchair too regal for rocking.

They moved the next day to a more modest hotel: the Princess Caroline. It was tucked in a quieter arrondissement, near bakeries that opened at dawn and smelled like comfort. The hotel had flower boxes on every window and a lobby desk manned by a woman who wore her disapproval like lipstick.

Their room was smaller, with floral wallpaper and mismatched furniture, and it felt like home immediately. Judy exhaled the moment they stepped in. Jim plopped onto the bed and announced that the springs had "just enough give to let you live, but not enough to make you cocky."

The elevator was a highlight, an open latticework iron cage that moved at the pace of an existential crisis. The porter, a man who looked like he'd seen things and had opinions about all of them, hauled their luggage up three flights, one slow stair at a time.

"C'est lent, n'est-ce pas?" Judy asked, trying her remembered French.

The man grunted. "Oui, Madame. Descend not. It will be… fast."

They took the stairs down for the rest of the trip.

***

Mornings in Paris became a rhythm: Jim left early to scout breakfast while Judy stayed behind to negotiate with Jimmie's digestive schedule. He returned each time with croissants and stories from boulangeries where the line moved like a Catholic mass: slow, reverent, and occasionally interrupted by incense.

One morning, Jim returned to find Judy in deep negotiations with the bidet. "Is this… for babies?"

"I don't think so," Jim said, cradling a coffee that smelled like burnt wisdom.

"I mean, what if it is? The height is suspicious."

"It's not. Don't."

They compromised by using it to wash onesies.

In the afternoons, they took long walks. Jim carried the stroller like a siege engine over cobblestones, while Judy wore Jimmie in a wrap and tried to pretend she wasn't leaking through her shirt.

That week in Paris became legend within their small family. They visited the Louvre, taking turns pushing Jimmie in his buggy down marbled hallways filled with art older than anyone they'd ever met. Judy whispered bits of trivia and translation into Jim's ear, and he whispered jokes back, some of which were funny.

They ate street crepes on a park bench near the Seine. Jimmie chewed on one corner of a napkin and looked deeply unimpressed by Notre-Dame.

One evening, they sat outside a café in Montmartre, watching artists sketch tourists and pigeons in equal measure. Jim was sipping a martini that cost more than dinner on base. Judy fed Jimmie mashed carrots from a small jar.

"I think this is the best anniversary I've ever had," she said.

Jim grinned. "It's the only anniversary you've ever had."

"Well," she said, "high bar, then."

They watched the sun set over Paris, leaning into the warmth of each other and the chaos they had created. They were too young, too poor, and completely in over their heads.

And completely in love.

***

The final night in Paris, they wandered the lit streets with no destination. Jimmie had finally fallen asleep, swaddled tight in his buggy like a diplomat.

Jim stopped in front of a bookshop with a display of French poetry. He picked up a volume and flipped through it.

"Any of this make sense to you?"

Judy took it. "Bits. Enough."

"Read me something."

She skimmed and chose a short verse by Jacques Prévert. Her voice was soft, deliberate:

"Et chaque matin je te retrouve encore, Malgré la nuit, les guerres, les silences, les départs…"

"And every morning I find you again," she translated. "Despite the night, the wars, the silences, the departures…"

Jim nodded, looking at her as if memorizing her face.

"That's us," he said.

She leaned her head on his shoulder. "That's us."

***

The trip home was quieter. Paris had wrung them out in the best way. The little gray VW hummed through the countryside, the jerry cans clinking softly on the roof.

At a roadside café in Alsace, they stopped for coffee and Jimmie's now-routine diaper change. An elderly woman smiled and pinched Jimmie's cheeks.

"Trés beau garçon," she said.

Jim raised a brow. "What's that?"

"Very handsome boy."

"Well, she's not wrong."

They returned to Nellingen sunburned, happy, and just slightly more worldly. The apartment, cramped and familiar, greeted them like an old friend.

They unpacked slowly, each item a tiny story now, paper napkins with Eiffel Towers on them, a broken toy from a street vendor, the poetry book wrapped in Judy's scarf.

Later that night, as Jim placed a sleepy Jimmie into his crib, Judy leaned in the doorway.

"You know," she said, "we're going to remember this week forever."

Jim nodded. "Because it was perfect?"

"No. Because it was ours."

He smiled. "Same thing."

Outside, the summer night was quiet, and the world kept turning. But inside their little apartment, it felt, for one long breath, as if it had stopped, just long enough for the three of them to hold it in their hands.

Chapter 5

It was June, of course, who fell in love with the Volkswagen. "So *posh*, so *sensible*," she announced one afternoon, standing beside it in the barracks courtyard as if admiring a beloved grandchild at a school recital. She took it for a spin once around the perimeter of the military housing complex, very nearly into a hedge, and came back flushed with triumph and possibly fear. "I simply must have one," she declared, clutching her handbag like it might help with gear shifts.

Jim suggested she wire the money and they'd see to it that one arrived safely at her front door or at least the curb. "We'll drive it to Hamburg," he said, "the Army'll ship it back. One less thing to worry about."

"And if it goes missing at sea?" June asked, narrowing her eyes suspiciously, as if Jim might personally pilot it into the Atlantic.

"Then at least it died a good death," Judy replied, patting the bonnet.

The arrangement was made. The money was wired. Jim drove the VW to Hamburg with military paperwork in triplicate and a thermos of very bad coffee. It was shipped with what he later described as "a surprisingly formal goodbye," and a salute from a German dockworker who may or may not have been joking.

But with the VW gone, they were left, briefly, with only feet, trains, and the will of God. And yet, there was an itch. A vehicular itch.

They had, of course, looked at the Porsche. Who wouldn't? A machine built like a bar of soap, sleek and fast and wholly unaffordable. They stood in a showroom for nearly eleven minutes, inhaling leather and fiscal reality. Jim did the math in silence. Judy squinted at the price tag as though it might blink.

"We could sell a kidney," Jim offered.

"Only if it comes with a mechanic," Judy replied, and they left.

The Triumph was a more familiar beast. Jim had owned a TR3 before they'd married and joined the Army, back when his hair did as it was told and his shoes weren't government-issued. The TR4 was its grown-up cousin, a little broader in the shoulders, a touch more refined, but still irrepressibly American. It had charm. It had history. It also had a rather limited color palette.

And so, they compromised: a non-standard paint job, Porsche dark blue, naturally, which Triumph accepted for an additional $600. "It's entirely reasonable," Jim said, which was the sort of thing one says when logic has lost to vanity. The collection point? Coventry, England.

"Well," Judy said, folding the travel map like an origami swan, "we've always wanted to see England."

There followed a series of increasingly charming forms of transportation. First, a train, efficient, if lacking in conversation. Then the ferry across the English Channel, which pitched and rolled with the enthusiasm of a toddler on a trampoline. Judy was pale. Jim was stoic. Jimmie was absolutely fine.

"He's either a born sailor," Judy muttered into a damp paper bag, "or not bright enough to notice we're moving."

"Portent of things to come," Jim said, watching Jimmie clap delightedly at the snack cart.

Once safely on British soil, they continued by train to Coventry: quieter, older, and smelling vaguely of soot and scones. The factory itself was a curious mix of industrial sprawl and warm civility. They were met at the gate by a man in a tie, who shook Jim's hand with great ceremony and addressed Judy as "Madam," which made her instantly forgive the ferry.

Lunch was provided: roast beef, boiled potatoes, and a steamed pudding that might have predated the War. They ate in a modest canteen with walls painted a color best described as "1948 Linoleum" and a portrait of Her Majesty watching over them with the mild expression of someone who never personally had to eat custard from a tin.

Then came the main event.

The warehouse was vast and echoing, the sort of place where sound traveled thoughtfully. Their new car sat in the center like a guest of honor at a wedding, gleaming dark blue, its surface catching the light in a way that seemed almost smug. Around it stood four or five men in suits, not speaking, just… admiring.

"Well," Judy whispered. "Looks like we weren't the only ones seduced by color swatches."

Jim approached first, nodded gravely at the men, and walked a slow circle around the car. One of the suits finally broke the silence.

"You've done something rather remarkable," he said. "That color…it's an exact match for the blue in the Triumph crest."

There was a pause.

"We hadn't noticed," Jim lied.

They were photographed with the car. Tea was served again. The color, they were told, would be added to next year's standard options. "You've set a trend," the factory man beamed.

Jim later wrote in his notebook: "Triumph now comes in American vanity."

They drove the new car out of Coventry that afternoon, its engine purring with the composed dignity of a well-bred English butler: quiet, confident, and just faintly disapproving of anyone who questioned its pedigree. The steering was crisp, the acceleration swift but never vulgar, and the leather interior still carried the scent of craftsmanship and faintly of pipe tobacco, as if the spirit of some retired colonel had blessed it at the factory gates. Judy strapped Jimmie into the back seat, wedged gently between two pillows and a duffel bag of emergency nappies, and they set off down the wrong side of the road with only mild screaming.

Their first stop: a petrol station run by a man who seemed personally offended by their accents.

Their second: a countryside inn where Jimmie was declared "a robust little chap" by the barmaid and Jim was served a pint of something entirely undrinkable but very patriotic.

They fell in love with England slowly and without resistance. The villages. The hedgerows. The fact that no one made eye contact unless absolutely necessary. The car, of course, fit right in. People nodded at it approvingly at traffic lights. Children pointed. A constable gave them a warning for "spirited acceleration" outside Oxford and then asked if he might look under the bonnet.

By the time they returned to Germany, the car was less a purchase and more a character in their lives. It had personality. Swagger. A boot that refused to close unless coaxed with flattery and violence. So yes, life was good.

***

By autumn, Europe had changed her dress again. The forests darkened. The Alps bristled. And the air in southern Germany had begun to whisper of winter. For Jim and Judy, stationed in Nellingen with baby Jimmie now a seasoned traveler, the looming end of Jim's military tour offered a narrow window for one final, ambitious trip. Italy beckoned. It had the irresistible charm of crumbling columns, chaotic scooters, and the kind of history that made even well-behaved toddlers seem like a manageable risk.

Jim had recently declined an offer to "re-up" and extend his Army career. The reassignment had been described in vague, administrative tones as a posting to "Southeast Asia," which sounded, at the time, like an exotic but unnecessary detour. They would learn later, with a shiver of retrospective gratitude, that it meant Vietnam. No, thank you. They would rather take their chances with Roman traffic.

The timing had to be precise. Jim was involved in implementing a new military supply system, an undertaking that combined logistics, diplomacy, and low-grade chaos. He had carved out a few precious vacation days with surgical precision, determined not to leave behind a warehouse full of misrouted canned peaches.

Jimmie had proven himself a decent traveler during earlier trips to France and England. He regarded new surroundings with the serene detachment of a visiting dignitary, occasionally bestowing smiles or tantrums as the mood struck him. So the little family packed up their new TR4, still glowing in its custom Porsche-blue paint, with only a faint patina of baby snack dust, and set off southward.

Their first day out of Munich began with optimism and wool scarves. The Triumph purred through Bavarian countryside, its engine humming like a well-bred baritone. But barely 150 miles into the trip, the autobahn came to a standstill. Traffic was frozen, not metaphorically, but literally. A multi-car accident up ahead had snarled the route, the icy conditions transforming the normally merciless autobahn into a treacherous, slow-moving chessboard.

They idled quietly, the windows fogging. Judy was unwrapping a banana for Jimmie, who showed early signs of disliking German bananas, when Jim glanced into the rearview mirror.

What he saw was a study in inevitability: a car behind them, gaining momentum with tragic grace, was skidding downhill toward their stationary Triumph. The driver's eyes were wide. The tyres had long given up pretending to grip the road.

There was nothing to do but watch.

Time slowed. The car continued to approach, its deceleration maddeningly incremental. What felt like an entire opera's worth of time passed before the moment of contact. The crash itself was neither explosive nor violent, just a sickening jolt, a crunch of metal on metal, and the peculiar sound of Judy whispering a curse so polite it might've been mistaken for a prayer.

The damage to the TR4 was significant but not catastrophic. The rear was crumpled, but the wheels were straight and the engine unbothered. After extricating themselves from the car, Jim exchanged insurance information with the rattled driver while a Polizei officer arrived, took notes with clipped precision, and filed a report that likely still exists in some drawer in Munich.

They found a modest hotel for the night, carrying in Jimmie, who had slept through both the accident and the aftermath with the serenity of a monk. The next morning, their spirits slightly creased but not folded, they turned their attention to finding a repair shop. Explaining their predicament involved a mix of English, gestures, and the universal language of pointing at a bent fender with a pained expression.

Miraculously, the mechanics at the shop responded with the kind of brisk efficiency that only Germans and obsessive watchmakers can muster. They nodded, frowned thoughtfully at the vehicle, and promised it back the next day. Judy blinked. "Really?"

"Ja," the man replied. "We don't like broken things."

Freed from automotive purgatory, they took a tram into Munich that evening and visited the famed Hofbräuhaus, where tourists, locals, and professional drinkers gathered beneath beer hall chandeliers and oompah music rolled through the rafters like weather. Jim nursed a litre of something dark and bitter; Judy raised a glass to missed wars and postponed plans. Jimmie, ever adaptable, gnawed contentedly on a giant pretzel and watched the brass band with open skepticism.

The following afternoon, true to their word, the repair shop returned the Triumph with its rear end repaired and its pride mostly intact. The Porsche-blue paint was untouched. The lines were still elegant. The damage, much like the memory of the crash, had faded just enough to seem like a footnote.

Their itinerary had taken a hit, Rome and Naples would now be approached with a more fluid sense of scheduling, but the road south still waited. They climbed back into the car, strapped Jimmie in, and resumed the rhythm of travel. The TR4, once again humming with faint nobility, rolled forward toward the promise of espresso and ancient ruins.

The car was no longer perfect. But then, neither were they. And that, Jim thought, was all the more reason to keep going. And so they were off to Italy.

***

Evening always brought a gentle kind of mystery in Italy. As the day's golden light surrendered to dusk, each town shimmered with a soft glow, ancient cobbled streets winding past shuttered windows and half-laughed conversations. No two evenings were quite the same, yet in every new place, one thing remained remarkably consistent: Jimmie was welcomed as if he were the mayor's cherished grandson.

They'd no sooner take a table at a trattoria than a kind-faced waitress would lean over, hands clasped in maternal delight.

"Posso portarlo un momento?" she'd ask, gesturing toward the child with a glance that sought permission and already knew it would be granted.

"Just for a short time," Judy would reply, amused, though she never quite knew where he was off to.

"Only to the kitchen," the waitress would assure, sweeping the boy gently into her arms and disappearing behind the swinging doors.

The first time it happened, Judy's maternal instincts kicked in with a flicker of alarm, but then came the sounds, chefs calling out greetings in sing-song Italian, a burst of laughter, and, moments later, Jimmie's delighted coo. Soon it became a beloved ritual. He'd return smelling faintly of garlic and basil, proudly bearing a breadstick or a flour-dusted smile. The Italians, with their deep-rooted reverence for family, embraced him without hesitation. In some corners of Tuscany and Lazio, he was no doubt remembered as the traveling cherub with American shoes and an old soul.

With Jimmie content and entertained, Jim and Judy found rare pockets of calm, an unhurried glass of wine, a second helping of osso buco, or even a brief conversation without interruption. On one occasion, Jim scanned the wine list and pointed vaguely.

"Chianti, per favore."

The waiter raised an eyebrow. "Rosato?"

Jim frowned. His brain, still tuned to German after more than a year in Stuttgart, misheard. "Grossa?" he repeated, shaking his head. "No, no. Small is fine."

The waiter gave a courteous nod and returned with a chilled bottle of Chianti Bianco, white Chianti. A Tuscan specialty they'd never even heard of, let alone tasted. Judy sipped, smiled, and raised her glass.

"Well," she said. "Every day's a school day."

After dinner, they often strolled the piazzas with Jimmie tucked in his sling, fountains whispering behind them and church bells marking the hour. But soon, they were back on the road.

The Via Roma unfolded before them like a ribbon, meandering along cliffsides and through olive groves. The TR4 handled it with grace, its engine humming in harmony with the curves. For Jim, who still mourned his beloved TR3 from his bachelor days, this car was redemption with a bit more polish. And he wasn't the only one enjoying it.

One afternoon, somewhere along the coast between Genoa and Pisa, a sleek Alfa Romeo appeared in the rearview mirror, a dashing fellow in driving gloves and a scarf trailing in the wind.

"He's eyeing us," Jim muttered with a grin.

"Let him try," Judy said, pretending to check her reflection in the mirror but actually watching the car's every move.

The Alfa lingered, dancing in and out of view. Jim began playing with the gearbox, seven forward speeds in total, thanks to Triumph's clever addition of overdrive on second, third, and fourth gears. He navigated the hairpins with the finesse of a Le Mans driver, pushing just enough to keep the Italian intrigued but behind.

The Alfa's driver eventually pulled alongside at a scenic overlook, both cars pausing in mutual admiration. The man tipped his cap, and Jim returned the gesture with mock solemnity.

"Bravo," the man said.

Jimmie, snoozing in the back jump seat, had slept through the entire chase, lulled by the rhythm of the road and the warm Italian sun.

And then, Rome.

The Eternal City didn't just reveal herself; she confronted them, bold and glorious and maddeningly tangled. Their map, folded, scribbled on, and possibly upside down, told them the hotel was just past the Trevi Fountain. But the lanes, in true Roman style, shifted without warning, like living things. They missed their turn.

"We'll have to circle," Judy sighed.

"Or orbit," Jim muttered, already halfway through what felt like a chariot race around a dozen unmarked roundabouts.

Eventually, they found their street and the hotel, pulling into what appeared to be a modest, set-back drive. But modesty, it seemed, was misleading. The descent was bumpy, almost cobbled, and then, abruptly, they were *in* the hotel lobby.

Not beside it. Not under it. *In it.*

Guests froze mid-conversation. A waiter stopped pouring coffee. A bell rang faintly from a reception desk as if to mark their arrival.

The porter approached without blinking, trained for emergencies and Americans alike.

"Benvenuti," he said, without irony.

Jim, in a masterclass of British restraint, climbed out, handed over the keys, and declared, "Checking in. Do be careful with the clutch. It's still quite tender."

He popped the boot and opened the door for Judy, who stepped out with Jimmie like they did this sort of thing every Tuesday.

The next day brought the requisite pilgrimage to St. Peter's Basilica, a marvel of light and grandeur that somehow even the TR4 respected. They parked just beside the colonnades, unbothered by any security presence.

Jim grinned. "Another holy nappy change."

Judy nodded solemnly. "May the child be blessed. And dry."

Inside, the basilica rose like a sacred forest, columns stretching skyward, art flowing in gold and stone. They joined a small congregation at a side altar where a priest quietly prepared for mass. Judy held Jimmie close. He didn't fuss. Didn't cry. He gazed upward at the frescoed ceiling, as if drinking in Michelangelo's vision, his wide eyes reflecting the blues and ochres of the Last Judgement.

A woman nearby leaned over and whispered, "Bellissimo bambino."

Judy smiled. "He knows he's somewhere special."

They stood, not speaking, as the incense curled and the light filtered in through ancient stained glass. Jim thought of all the places they'd been, all the turns they'd taken, literal and otherwise, and of the chance they had turned down months earlier.

The 2.5-hour drive south to Naples unspooled like a ribbon of time, each mile drawing them deeper into the warmth and mystery of southern Italy. The Mediterranean air grew thicker with the scent of salt and citrus, and the buildings wore their sun-faded pastels like memory itself: soft, cracked, enduring. But the true highlight of the journey came when they veered off the highway and entered the ancient city of Pompeii.

The ruins stretched before them in sun-bleached stone and volcanic ash, a quiet city frozen in the shadow of catastrophe. They wandered the narrow streets of a place where life had been so abruptly stilled, past frescoes that still bled pigment after nearly two millennia and courtyards that once rang with children's laughter. For Jim, it was staggering, the immediacy of it all. The homes still told their stories. Clay jars, stone beds, household shrines, it was all there, abandoned in motion, waiting. He imagined the moment the sky darkened and the mountain roared.

Jimmie, of course, was too young to grasp the weight of history, but he became the center of a smaller drama. At one excavated home, Judy had the idea to place him, carefully and safely, inside a wide clay storage jar, just for a photograph. His red knit hat peeked out like a cherry on a relic sundae, his head centered perfectly inside the wide mouth of the amphora. Tourists giggled nearby, and even the guards cracked a smile, until one stepped forward with furrowed brows and a finger raised in warning. "Signora, the baby, please. He disturbs the ruin." They quickly lifted Jimmie out, apologizing and brushing off bits of ancient dust from his clothes. Later, they laughed about it in the car: *Jimmie ruining the ruins.*

But beneath the humor, Jim remained quietly awed. Pompeii was a city silenced mid-sentence. The plaster casts of voids where bodies once lay, the graffiti on the walls, the loaf of bread still in the oven of a bakery, all spoke with astonishing clarity. Here was life, paused in terror, preserved by fire and ash. Jim found himself thinking about the scale of time. Just hours ago, they had stood under the vaulted dome of St. Peter's Basilica, a monument built 1,500 years *after* this city was buried. Standing here, among the ghosted remnants of 79 AD, he felt history not as a distant concept but as something alive and close.

As the sun dipped lower, casting golden light over broken columns and dusty cobblestones, they knew it was time to turn north. The week was drawing to a close, and Stuttgart, home for now, called them back.

But Italy wasn't done with them yet.

They made a deliberate stop in Florence, determined to pay their respects to Michelangelo's David. The statue stood beneath its dome in the Accademia, marble muscle and tension immortalized in a pose of alert calm. Jim stared up, humbled by the precision of it. Judy held Jimmie in her arms as they circled the base slowly. For a moment, it felt as if they weren't just visiting places, they were touching greatness.

By contrast, Pisa was a blink. They drove through without stopping, the Leaning Tower flashing briefly through the car window like a postcard someone else had written. No photos. No climbing. Just a passing nod to one of the world's most iconic architectural accidents. As they laughed at their own haste, Judy teased, "We've officially become the tourists we swore we'd never be."

The final leg home was quiet. Jimmie napped in the back, lulled by the engine's hum. Jim watched the lines of the autobahn unwind before them. A car ride through ancient lands, a clay pot moment in Pompeii, and a silent child in Michelangelo's chapel. It had been the right choice.

Chapter 6

As their tour of duty neared its end, a strange tension settled into the days, a mix of anticipation and unspoken dread. They were desperate to return to the States, to the promise of routine and solid ground, but also to finally place Jimmie into the arms of the family who had only known him in black-and-white photographs and carefully worded letters. For Jim's parents, who had followed every update like scripture, the idea of meeting their grandson in the flesh felt almost too good to be true. That longing, stretching across time zones and sea miles, had begun to feel like gravity, pulling them home.

Then came the offer. A chance for Jim to extend his military service, but this time it was without Judy. Southeast Asia. Vietnam. It was brief, almost casual, like the flick of a coin. Accept, and the next chapter would be written in jungle heat and radio static. Decline, and step back into civilian life. Jim said no. Maybe it was instinct. Maybe it was something deeper, a primal refusal to risk never seeing his family again. The enormity of that decision was invisible at the time, cloaked in daily distractions. But in hindsight, it stood like a fork in the road, with one path disappearing into darkness.

With the war behind them, for now, they turned their focus to the journey home. Jim looked forward to returning to Union Special, the company that had held his job open with rare loyalty. But first, there was the scramble of endings: furniture to sort and pack, bureaucratic hurdles to clear, and the sleek new TR4 to deliver to the port for shipment. Their last days in Europe moved quickly, the logistics like a fast-moving tide carrying them toward an inevitable departure.

The Army arranged for Judy and Jimmie to travel by military transport ship. Jim's final task was both simple and unbearable: get them to the port, see them aboard, and say goodbye, for now. The USNS General Maurice Rose loomed large and gray in the misty harbor, its name painted in bold letters that made it feel almost noble. Jim walked them up the gangplank and saw them settled into an officer's cabin, a small mercy that offered some privacy amid the steel and salt.

Then he turned and walked away, his boots echoing on the dock. He wouldn't see them again until they were back on American soil.

The crossing was brutal. March in the North Atlantic showed no mercy. Icy winds howled against the hull like banshees, and waves rose up like mountains, slamming into the ship with merciless rhythm. Seasickness swept through the decks like wildfire, reducing most passengers to pale, groaning bundles curled in their bunks. But not Judy. And not Jimmie.

Somehow, the baby remained calm, and Judy, calm-eyed and steady, managed with the quiet resilience that had become her signature. One afternoon, as the dining room echoed with the clatter of plates and the groans of the sea, a rogue wave struck the ship broadside. The double doors to the dining room burst open, and a wall of freezing seawater surged in, flooding the floor.

Most had already retreated to their cabins. But Judy and Jimmie were there, in the near-empty room, stubbornly clinging to a rhythm of normalcy. As the cold water swirled around their feet, Judy scooped Jimmie into her arms, propped her legs on the chair's metal rungs, and waited. Calm, composed, soaked. When the kitchen staff rushed in, she greeted them not with panic, but a polite nod, her voice steady despite the chaos. The sea, it seemed, would not get the better of her either.

Meanwhile, Jim had crossed the ocean above the clouds. Aboard a military transport plane, he flew through turbulence of a different kind, his thoughts clouded with worry, his future still taking shape. He was officially discharged at Fort Dix, New Jersey, the Army releasing him back into a world that had moved on without him. The TR4 had already arrived at port, and he retrieved it with an odd sense of detachment, the glossy British sports car looking almost surreal in the American sunlight.

Days later, he stood at the Brooklyn Navy Yard, scanning the arriving passengers for a familiar silhouette. Then there they were. Judy, windblown and weary, but upright. Jimmie in her arms, blinking at the brightness. They had crossed the sea and come out the other side.

Home. Not all at once, not in the way they'd imagined it, but they were home.

Back in Chicago, they stepped into a liminal space, a return that felt both deeply familiar and curiously alien. Judy's parents, June and Bill, opened their doors and their arms, offering more than just a roof; they offered a landing place, a soft corner of the world where the sharp edges of transition could begin to dull. The war was behind them now, yet its shadows lingered in the corners of every room. The rhythm of their new life had yet to settle.

Jim shed his uniform with a quiet finality and returned to Union Special in downtown Chicago, slipping back into the civilian current with a new sense of gravity. Each morning, he knotted his tie with the practiced hand of a man who had once laced combat boots, his movements brisk, his eyes tired. On the surface, the change seemed seamless. But under the surface, the shift was tectonic: soldier to civilian, father to provider, wanderer to anchor.

Judy, meanwhile, was standing at her own kind of crossroads. Her secondary education degree, carefully preserved through wartime chaos, was her talisman, a promise that her life could stretch beyond kitchens and cribs. She didn't just want to teach; she needed to. It was a hunger for identity, for relevance, for something wholly her own. Her resumes were dispatched like tiny flares into the unknown, each one stitched with quiet hope.

But Jimmie needed care. Real, loving, patient care from someone who saw him not just as a task but as a trust.

June was already committed to her post at the Cook County Highway Department, steering through bureaucratic mazes and city maps. Bill, ever reliable, climbed poles for Bell Telephone, threading the city's voices through coils of copper and static. Their lives were full, their time accounted for.

And so, the role fell naturally and inevitably to Mother.

Jim's grandmother wasn't just family; she was steel in an apron. Her hands had raised generations, her voice could part a room, and her gaze had the quiet weight of command. She didn't ask for respect. She emanated it. She would not babysit Jimmie; she would raise him. She would guard his days with the same unwavering vigilance that she'd given to her own children, and their children after them. And in truth, there had never been anyone else they'd trusted more.

They scoured neighborhoods for an apartment near her home with the kind of urgency reserved for life-and-death decisions. It had to be close, close enough for her to arrive each morning before the city yawned awake. It had to be accessible to the expressway, where Jim's British-made TR4 would growl like a lion into the twilight, a mechanical lullaby that told Jimmie: *Daddy's home.*

But the future, as always, had its fists half-clenched.

Judy's job hunt became a battlefield. Every high school door she knocked on looked her up and down, not at her credentials, not at her enthusiasm, but at her womb. A woman of childbearing age, they said, posed a "distraction" to adolescent boys. As if her mind, her voice, her ambition were footnotes to the threat of her biology. They turned her away with smiles so polished they reflected their own hypocrisy.

It was more than rejection. It was erasure.

And yet Judy did not fold. She turned, with dignity and quiet fury, to the primary schools. There, the scrutiny was softer, or at least cloaked in kinder language. Her warmth, her intellect, her conviction, all of it spoke louder than prejudice could whisper. Within weeks, she was hired.

Not because she asked for a chance.

Because she *was* the chance.

And so, their new apartment absorbed them like a lung drawing breath: quietly, steadily, until it held the shape of their lives. Jim's parents had outfitted Jimmie's nursery with loving precision: a crib painted soft white, a maple dresser that smelled faintly of lemon oil, linens folded with the same care once reserved for christening gowns. The walls, still echoing with fresh paint, slowly surrendered to the sounds of new life, Jimmie's high-pitched laughter, the staccato thump of toddler footsteps, the sharp cry that sliced through midnight and summoned comfort without hesitation. Even the air seemed to change, thick with the invisible pulse of a family claiming space and purpose.

Through every upheaval, forests, storms, foreign ports, Jimmie had been an island of calm. His world, though ever shifting, remained solid as long as Judy and Helmut were near. Helmut, their oddball German cat with the spine of a soldier and the soul of a nurse, had become Jimmie's shadow. Wherever the boy went, the cat followed, part guardian, part ghost. He perched near the crib like a sentinel, ears flicking at every whimper, tail twitching in tune with the baby's breath. The U.S. Army had seen fit to fund Helmut's return too, his travel documents stamped and sealed like a dignitary's. The cat, Judy often joked, came home with more ceremony than they had, complete with a layover dinner in Paris. Passport, pedigree, and now, permanent resident of Chicago's hardwood floors.

Before dawn each morning, Mother arrived like a metronome, precise and unsentimental. Her coat buttoned to the collar, eyes sharp, presence commanding without ever raising her voice. She tended to Jimmie, yes, but also to everything else: unwashed dishes, rumpled shirts, Judy's forgotten breakfast. Her care flowed into every crack, filling what the young parents couldn't name, much less ask for.

One morning, Jim dressed in the dark, careful not to stir Judy. Hours later, in the fluorescent hush of a downtown office bathroom, he glanced down and froze. His boxers: paisley, flamboyant, utterly foreign.

Not his. Not even close. For a split second, panic flared. Had he lost his mind? Sleptwalked into another man's drawer?

Judy solved it with a laugh that evening. Mother had noticed his threadbare supply and simply… acted. Bought replacements, folded them into his drawer, never thought to mention it. In her world, things that needed doing got done. No discussion, no fuss. If she could anticipate even that, what did that say about the devotion she poured into Jimmie?

That spring was a fragile marvel. Their days were tacked together not with certainty, but with the quiet heroism of showing up. A secondhand crib. A job hard-won. A sports car's low growl announcing Jim's return. A great-grandmother's silent hand smoothing the creases of their days. It was messy. It was mundane. It was a kind of magic.

Chapter 7

Chicago had a way of swallowing men whole. Its streets thundered with the weight of trains, trucks, and ambition; its skyline clawed at the sky with stone and steel. When Jim returned with Judy and little Jimmie, it was not as the boy who had once tested his wings here, but as a man with a family depending on his ascent.

The Union Special factory still pulsed northwest of the city, its windows glowing like a shipyard at dusk, but Jim no longer belonged to the shop floor. His training had shifted, carrying him each morning into the Loop, where the company's downtown offices loomed in glass and stone. To Jim, that tower felt like a citadel, a place where men's careers were forged, defended, or lost.

The drive from Dolton stretched long, an hour each way, sometimes more, but Jim did not complain. Each morning, he slid behind the wheel of the Triumph TR4, the convertible's lines rakish against the river of gray sedans clogging the expressway. When the engine hummed, Jim felt younger, sharper, as if the car itself conspired with him against the drudgery of the commute. He liked to think of himself as cutting through the monotony, arriving not merely at work but at possibility.

Sometimes, Judy would watch from the porch as he backed down the drive, Jimmie perched at her hip. She'd wave, though her eyes followed the taillights with a trace of worry. The city consumed men; she hoped it would not consume her husband.

A year passed that way, twelve months measured in late-night reports, long drives, and Judy's careful tending of home and child. When Union Special summoned Jim for his next test, neither of them was surprised. The program was designed to scatter its young trainees like chessmen across the country, each to prove themselves on some distant board.

For Jim, the assignment was Boston.

The name carried weight. Boston was not just another market; it was a place where the cobblestones themselves whispered of revolution and tradition. It was old money, old families, old grudges, and yet, beneath all that, an industry as hungry as any in Chicago.

The phone call came from Bill Palm himself, the Boston office manager. His voice carried the warmth of seasoned authority.

"Jim," Bill said, "it's time you came east. Don't think of this as a posting. Think of it as an inheritance. Boston doesn't open easily, but once it does, you'll find it holds fast."

He insisted they come see the city, even booking them into the Parker House Hotel. Judy, though no stranger to flying after her earlier trip to Germany, still packed carefully, her hands trembling slightly as she folded Jimmie's clothes.

"Boston," she whispered to herself as she zipped the suitcase. "Boston." The word felt like a promise and a challenge, both.

The Parker House greeted them like a relic of another century. Its paneled halls glowed with mahogany and brass, and liveried staff moved with the precision of dancers. Jimmie, wide-eyed, clung to Judy's skirt as they crossed the marble lobby. Jim, trying to look worldly, whispered, "They've been serving those Parker House rolls since Lincoln was president."

Judy laughed, though she was too tired from the flight to fully take in the grandeur. Still, when the rolls came, warm, golden, endless, she admitted quietly, "I'll remember these long after I forget the wallpaper."

***

Bill and his wife, "Sis," met them that evening. They did not carry the stiffness Judy half-expected from New Englanders. Instead, their welcome came with open arms. Bill was a tall man, hair silvered at the temples, voice calm and certain. Sis, gracious and quick to smile, bent immediately to scoop Jimmie into her lap as if he were her own grandson.

"You'll find Boston a different rhythm," Bill told Jim over dinner. "Chicago runs on brawn. Boston runs on memory. Families here, especially in textiles, they don't trade accounts lightly. You're not selling them machines; you're joining their history."

Jim listened intently, absorbing every word as though they were scripture. Later, walking back to the hotel under the glow of gas-lit lamps, he admitted to Judy, "I've never met a man who seemed to know both business and people so well."

Judy squeezed his arm. "Then learn everything you can from him."

In the days that followed, Bill guided them through Boston with the ease of a man who knew every street, every hidden corner. They drove through neighborhoods where red-brick homes lined narrow streets, and through towns that still bore the stamp of their colonial past.

"This is not just geography," Bill explained as they passed Concord green. "This is identity. If you can understand a town's history, you'll understand how it buys, how it works, how it trusts."

For Judy, the city felt foreign yet magnetic. She pushed Jimmie's stroller through Boston Common, marveling at the swan boats and the gilded dome of the State House beyond. Life here seemed at once slower and older, but beneath that slowness she felt a taut thread of pride that made the air itself different from Chicago.

They soon found a place to live: a ground-floor apartment in Woburn, just northwest of the city. Two bedrooms, a walk-out patio, a small yard where Jimmie could tumble in the grass. When Judy first stepped into the empty rooms, sunlight streaming across bare floors, she closed her eyes and whispered, "It feels like ours."

The location was perfect, close to shops, parks, and church, but just far enough from the city's churn. Jim could reach the office without battle-weary commuting, and Judy could breathe in air that smelled of grass instead of soot.

It wasn't grand. But it was home. Their first real family home.

Practicality though demanded an adjustment as well: gone was the rakish TR4, sacrificed on the altar of responsibility, and in its place came a full-sized car, solid, respectable, a vehicle that announced not just a promotion but a settling into life's next chapter. It was the kind of car that befitted a young executive, broad enough to carry a family and steady enough to face New England winters without flinching. Yet the irony quickly revealed itself: the car became less Jim's possession than Bill's convenience. The manager often preferred Jim to drive him on customer visits, slipping into the passenger seat with a briefcase balanced on his lap, as if the car had always been intended for this purpose. Jim didn't mind; in fact, he relished it. To sit behind the wheel while Bill narrated the map of New England commerce was to receive an education no university could provide, names of men who mattered, the rise and fall of companies, the grudges carried from one generation to the next, all tumbling out as towns blurred past. Each highway exit was a lecture, each turnpike toll a new chapter. Jim the chauffeur listened carefully, knowing he was being invited into a world that was equal parts opportunity and obligation.

Boston itself, however, refused to yield so easily. If Chicago was a city laid out with a draftsman's ruler, streets stretching straight as equations, logic governing the very soil, Boston was something else entirely, a riddle wrapped in centuries of stone. Its streets looped and twisted with the stubbornness of memory, as if the old cow paths had hardened into granite and dared newcomers to make sense of them. For Jim, fresh to the city's pulse, it was maddening. More than once he found himself circling the same block, frustration mounting while Judy tried to soothe a fussing Jimmie in the back seat. Directions offered no salvation. Locals, with a hint of mischief in their voices, would answer his plea for the intersection of two streets with a smirk and the impossible question: "Which one?" In Boston, even geography was a trickster, and Jim realized that mastery of the city would not be granted, it would have to be earned.

For Judy, Boston meant another kind of shift, quieter but no less profound. She folded up her teaching career like a beloved coat laid aside for a new season, turning her full attention to Jimmie and the life that now pressed its weight and promise into her arms. Woburn, their first foothold in Massachusetts, offered her something she had not expected: community. A neighbor upstairs, with a little boy named Joey, became both companion and anchor. The two children forged a friendship in the parking-lot playground where swings creaked in the late-day wind and tennis courts echoed with the sharp, measured thwack of rackets. It was there, under the shade of ordinary afternoons, that Judy began to breathe into her new role, learning the rhythms of motherhood and finding, to her quiet relief, that belonging could grow in the most unassuming corners of the world.

And then there were the friendships that stitched past to present. Jim and Judy reconnected with Rick, Jim's old fraternity pledge son, and his wife Lynn, who lived in the seaside town of Beverly, just north of Boston. For Judy, who had known Rick from her school days as well, the reunion felt natural, as if time had only paused and now resumed at a familiar pace. Their sons, Eric and Jimmie, were nearly the same age, tumbling together in play until their laughter dissolved into drowsy silence and they were tucked into beds, cheeks still flushed from the evening's games. The adults lingered long after, a deck of bridge cards spread across the table, conversation flowing as steadily as wine, sometimes serious, sometimes lighthearted, until the night slipped well past its hour. The friendship grew so comfortable, so rooted, that formal invitations became unnecessary; doors opened without ceremony, visits unplanned and unhurried, the children charging ahead into play while their parents settled into the ease of kindred company.

In those days, Boston was more than a city to be endured, it was a proving ground, a test of adaptability and endurance, but also a stage where unexpected bonds took shape. Jim wrestled with its streets, Judy with its silences, and together they began to stitch themselves into its fabric, not seamlessly, but with threads strong enough to hold.

Rick's family home in Concord, Massachusetts, was no ordinary house. It stood on its quiet street like a relic conjured out of another century, with weathered clapboards, stubborn shutters that clung to their hinges, and wide-planked floors that still whispered with every footstep. The house breathed history. Neighbors often joked that it looked as though Ralph Waldo Emerson himself might stride out the front door or Louisa May Alcott could be glimpsed in an upstairs window, pen scratching furiously across the page. Tourists, deceived by its Colonial bones and proud silhouette, sometimes mistook it for a museum and wandered onto the porch as though admission were free, startled when Rick's mother would open the door with a bemused smile. It was not curated history, it was lived history, worn into the bannisters and hearthstones, infused into every corner of that home.

Lynn's family lived just twenty miles away in Lexington, a short drive but an immeasurable leap across memory, geography, and myth. To grow up between Concord and Lexington was to live, quite literally, in the cradle of revolution. The air itself seemed heavier there, perfumed not only with lilacs in spring but with memory of musket smoke and shouted orders, of men and boys who had died in those fields believing the world could be remade. For Rick and Lynn, the old battle roads were not tourist routes; they were childhood landmarks. For Jim and Judy, transplanted Midwesterners, this landscape was nothing short of electric, a living reminder that history was not distant but pressed right up against the present.

It was in this spirit that Rick and Lynn invited Jim, Judy, and little Jimmie to join them for Thanksgiving, a holiday that in New England seemed charged with a more solemn gravity than elsewhere. The table groaned beneath the weight of tradition: roast turkey golden and fragrant, mashed potatoes whipped into clouds, pumpkin pies cooling on the sill. Laughter and warmth filled the house, yet underneath it all was a sense of rootedness, of belonging to a place that had shaped a nation. After the feast, they bundled themselves into coats and spilled outside for a football game, Rick and Jim grinning like boys as they squared off once again, recalling their Knox College days. The competition was good-natured, their bodies no longer colliding with the reckless violence of youth but moving with an easy grace, the game less about victory and more about friendship, about keeping alive a fire that had once burned brightly on college fields.

But if Thanksgiving bound them with the intimacy of hearth and harvest, Patriots' Day bound them with history itself. April 19th was no ordinary date in Massachusetts. On that day, businesses shuttered, streets hushed, and the living paused to honor the dead who had once answered liberty's call. Rick's family insisted they all attend the ceremonies. At dawn, the townspeople gathered at the Congregational Church, the old wooden pews creaking beneath them, as though even the furniture remembered. Admission came with a peculiar condition: soldiers, past and present, were to wear their uniforms; civilians were asked to adorn themselves with something that spoke of patriotism, an armband, a ribbon, a flag pin. To enter that sanctuary was to step into an unbroken line of tradition, as if each man and woman had been summoned not only by civic duty but by the ghosts of those who had gone before.

The evening reached its crescendo with the reenactment of Paul Revere's ride. Outside, the April air was crisp, smelling faintly of damp earth and wood smoke. A rider, silhouetted against the twilight, galloped furiously down the road. The clatter of hooves on cobblestones echoed like gunfire, and as he drew near, the old church bell thundered, summoning townsfolk as it had in 1775. Jim, with little Jimmie balanced on one arm, was invited to take the rope himself. The bell cord was rough against his hand, the weight of it almost startling as he pulled, each toll shuddering through his body and into the marrow of his bones. The sound rippled across the town like an incantation, each note both a warning and a remembrance.

It was then that Rick, standing close beside him, leaned in with a remark pitched half in jest, half in history. "You know," he murmured, "this might be the first time a Catholic has rung that Congregational bell."

The words hung in the air, heavier than they seemed. Jim laughed, but softly, aware of what Rick meant. For generations, lines had been drawn here, between Catholic and Protestant, newcomer and established family, Irish immigrant and Yankee Puritan. Within living memory, Catholics had been barred from country clubs, shut out of business circles, and reminded, in the cruellest ink of newspaper classifieds, that only "White, Anglo-Saxon, Protestants need apply." Yet here he stood, a Catholic husband, holding his young son against his chest, ringing a bell that had once called only to another faith, another people.

It was a moment both intimate and monumental. The clang of that bell did not simply echo across Concord's green; it echoed across time. Jim could feel it, feel the tension between what had been excluded and what was now embraced, between the narrowness of the past and the widening arms of the present. For a heartbeat, he was not just a visitor, not just a friend at a family gathering; he was part of something larger, woven, however briefly, into the ongoing story of America itself.

Chapter 8

The Buick's chrome caught the fading light as they pulled away from Boston, the convertible top folded neatly behind them, the engine humming with a quiet pride, as if even the car knew it was new to the family. Jim drove with one hand on the wheel, his other drumming the dashboard, while Judy kept her eyes on the road ahead. Their son, little Jimmie, bounced in the back seat, full of restless joy.

"Settle down, tiger," Jim called over his shoulder.

But Jimmie was already standing, his small hands swinging on the crossbars that supported the canvas roof, pretending the Buick was a jungle gym. His laughter, high, sharp, uncontainable, whipped away in the wind.

"Jim," Judy said gently, "you'll have to stop him before he knocks himself out."

"Hey, buddy!" Jim twisted halfway around, his voice playful but firm. "This is a car, not the playground."

Reluctantly, Jimmie sank back into the seat, his curls bouncing into his eyes. "But Daddy, it feels like flying."

Judy's gaze softened, her hand brushing across her skirt. She loved that he could still find joy in the smallest things. The drive from Boston to Chicago was long, but Jim's spirits were so buoyant, full of anticipation for the wedding, for old friends that the miles seemed lighter.

They arrived late that evening at Mother's home, the stately house standing like a sentinel in the quiet suburban neighborhood. The porch light spilled across the steps as Mother opened the door, her arms already extended.

"Well, you're finally here!" she said, wrapping Judy in a hug before reaching for her grandson. "And look at you, Jimmie…my, how you've grown."

The days that followed carried a rhythm of family warmth mixed with obligations. Jim, though technically on leave, was obliged to stop in at Union Special. The company had allowed for transit time and even covered mileage, but duty was duty. A couple of mornings, he slipped into his suit, kissed Judy's cheek, and drove off to the office while she remained behind with Jimmie and Mother.

It was on the third day that the world shifted.

They were in the parlor, Judy folding laundry, Jimmie pushing a wooden car across the rug, his small voice murmuring sound effects. Ermina sat stiffly in the wingback chair, her eyes sharp with thought. She had been watching Jimmie for some time, her lips pressed in a thin, uneasy line.

At last, she spoke. Her voice, though steady, rang like a bell in the quiet room:

"This child is blind."

The words hung in the air, heavy, unshakable. Judy froze, a sheet clutched in her hands.

"What?" she whispered.

Jim, who had just stepped in from the porch, stopped midstride. "Ermina, that's… that's impossible. He sees. He plays."

Ermina shook her head. "I took him yesterday to the eye doctor. He confirmed it. Jimmie cannot see."

Judy's breath caught in her throat, the room suddenly shrinking around her. She looked at her son, her sweet, laughing boy, still sliding the toy car in crooked lines across the carpet. He did not glance up when she whispered his name.

"How… how could we not have noticed?" Judy's voice trembled. "We're his parents. We should have…"

Jim knelt by Jimmie, his hands on the boy's shoulders. "Son," he said softly. "Can you see Daddy?"

Jimmie tilted his head, the question seeming to confuse him. "I hear you," he said simply.

The silence that followed was worse than any shout.

***

That night, after Jimmie had been tucked into bed, Jim and Judy sat together in the guest room. The suitcase lay half-packed at their feet. Judy's hands twisted in her lap.

"Were we so self-centered?" she asked in a whisper. "So blind ourselves that we couldn't see his pain?"

Jim reached for her, but his voice cracked as he spoke. "We can't change what we missed. We can only fix what we know now. We'll find the best doctors. We'll find answers."

Judy's eyes glistened. "And if it's more than blindness? What if it's something we can't…" Her voice trailed away.

The next morning, Jim called Rick Killam, an old friend and trusted colleague. His voice, though steady, carried the weight of desperation.

"Rick," he said, gripping the receiver. "I need references…medical contacts in Boston. Pediatric ophthalmologists, the best you know."

Rick didn't hesitate. "Mass General. They'll know what to do."

And so, with the trip cut short, they returned eastward, the Buick now less a proud symbol of adventure and more a vessel carrying fear and urgency.

***

At Massachusetts General Hospital, the corridors smelled of antiseptic and hushed voices. Judy clutched Jimmie's hand as they walked, his small steps careful on the polished floors. Doctors came and went, asking questions, shining lights, taking notes.

It was finally Dr. William H. Sweet who gave them the truth. His eyes were kind but steady, his words clear and unforgiving.

"Your son has a craniopharyngioma…a tumor pressing on the optic nerve. Surgery is necessary. And it must be immediate."

Judy gasped softly, covering her mouth. Jim tightened his grip on the chair's armrest.

"Will he see again?" Jim asked.

Dr. Sweet's silence stretched, broken only by the distant echo of hospital footsteps. At last, he said, "We can remove the tumor. Every cell, if we are successful. But the optic nerve has already sustained severe damage. Sight may not return."

Jimmie, sitting on Judy's lap, pressed his small hand to his mother's cheek. "Why are you crying, Mommy?"

And Judy broke.

The corridors of Massachusetts General Hospital smelled of antiseptic and boiled coffee. Judy trailed her hand along the tiled wall as they followed the nurse deeper into the pediatric ward. Each fluorescent light above hummed faintly, as if echoing the nervous buzz in her chest. Jim walked beside her, jaw set, one arm locked stiffly against his side as though keeping his fear from spilling out.

"Jim and Judy?" A young intern stepped forward, clipboard in hand, his round glasses glinting in the overhead light. "Dr. Sweet will see you now."

The name still startled Judy. *Sweet.* What a gentle name for a man who dealt daily with the cruelties of the brain. She wished she could lean on the kindness his name promised, but she knew better. The chief neurosurgeon was brisk, brilliant, and utterly unflinching. They had learned that already.

Inside his office, stacks of journals and neatly ordered case notes filled every surface. A chalk diagram of a brain loomed on one wall, an unfinished lecture in waiting. Dr. Sweet stood near his desk, his white coat buttoned high. His eyes softened briefly when they fell on Jimmie, who clutched Judy's hand, but his voice carried no softness at all.

"The tumor is a craniopharyngioma," he began, sliding a thin folder across the desk. "Benign in classification, but malignant in effect. It presses on the optic nerve and has already destroyed function. It must be removed…immediately."

Jim's hand twitched against his thigh. "What happens if we wait?"

Sweet shook his head. "There is no waiting. Pressure on the brain increases daily. The blindness is irreversible without removal, and the tumor itself could kill him."

Judy tightened her hold on Jimmie's small fingers. "He's three years old," she whispered. "Three."

"I know." Sweet's eyes flicked toward her, briefly human, then back to the folder. "That is why we move quickly."

Jimmie squirmed on her lap, restless, unaware of the gravity in the room. "Mama, my feet are cold."

Judy stroked his hair, swallowing a sob. *How can I tell him what's about to happen?* He would go under bright lights, into strange hands, and wake changed forever. Perhaps alive, perhaps not.

∗∗∗

The days before surgery unfolded like a fever dream. They stayed in a cramped hotel near the hospital, the city roaring around them with its trolley bells and clattering traffic. Judy found herself awake at night, staring at the ceiling fan's slow circle, hearing only her own thoughts: *What if he doesn't wake up? What if I never hear his laugh again? What if… what if…*

Jim, restless as ever, walked the streets until dawn, the soles of his shoes worn thin. He returned with his collar damp from fog and his eyes rimmed red, but he never spoke of his wandering. When Judy pressed, he muttered only, "I just need air."

The morning of the surgery, Judy faced those long hospital hours largely on her own, her mother unable to be in Boston during the operation.

One afternoon, seeking a moment's relief from the weight of hospital corridors, they stood together on the banks of the Charles River. Across from Mass General, Harvard's racing shells skimmed the water with swift precision, oars flashing in unison. For a little while, the rhythm of the rowers offered a lighter counterpoint to the heaviness of those days, a reminder that life carried on with grace and motion even in the midst of worry.

***

When the orderlies wheeled Jimmie away, his small figure swallowed by white sheets, Judy pressed her hand to the glass window of the swinging doors. He looked back once, confused, and called, "Mama?"

She smiled through tears. "I'll be right here, sweetheart."

The words tasted like lies.

The surgery lasted hours. The waiting room clock ticked so slowly Judy thought time itself had broken. Around them, life carried on: a mother comforting her coughing infant, a man pacing while muttering prayers into his rosary, nurses gliding in and out with clipboards. Jim sat hunched, elbows on his knees, silent for once. Every so often he clenched his fist against his lips, as though physically holding back the fear.

At last, Dr. Sweet appeared. His face was calm, unreadable. Judy leapt to her feet.

"Well?" she demanded, her voice breaking.

"It was successful," Sweet said simply. "Every cell removed. No regrowth expected."

Her knees nearly gave way. Relief surged so strong it was almost pain. Jim gripped her arm, steadying them both.

But Sweet wasn't finished. He glanced at the floor before continuing. "The pituitary gland was destroyed. Permanently. He will require lifelong hormonal replacement. Growth hormone, thyroid, adrenal support. Without it…he would not survive."

Judy blinked, the words sinking like stones. *Lifelong. Permanently. Not survive.*

"And his sight?" Jim's voice cracked.

Sweet shook his head. "The optic nerve is irreparably damaged. Blindness is complete. Though, given his age, there remains a remote chance of partial recovery. But you must be prepared…it may never come."

For a long moment, no one breathed. Then Jim whispered, "God help us."

***

The weeks of recovery tested them all. Jimmie whimpered constantly, his small hands fluttering in the air as if searching for the light he could no longer see. "Mama, where are you?" he asked again and again, even when Judy was holding him.

"I'm here, love," she said, her throat raw. "Always here."

At night, he complained of cold feet, his body shivering under hospital blankets. Judy tucked the covers tighter, rubbed his legs, begged the nurses for extra warmth. Jim stood helpless at the bedside, his usual bluster gone.

And always, there were the interns. Bright-eyed, eager, notebooks in hand. They swarmed the room like bees, firing questions, scribbling notes. "At what point did you first notice the blindness?" one asked. "Were there behavioral changes before diagnosis?" another pressed.

Judy bristled. "He's not a specimen," she snapped once. "He's our son."

But still they came, day after day, their curiosity endless. And she knew, deep down, that this case was rare, that Jimmie was already part of medical history whether she wanted it or not.

***

One night, when exhaustion pressed so heavily on her chest she thought she might collapse, Judy slipped down to the hospital chapel. It was dim, the only light coming from a row of votive candles flickering against the stained glass. She knelt awkwardly, her hands clasped so tight they hurt.

"Please," she whispered into the silence. "Please, let him live. I'll bear anything, just let him live."

Her voice broke, but she stayed there, rocking gently on her knees, until the candles blurred into halos of gold.

***

When Jimmie was finally discharged, the family left Mass General altered forever. Jim walked beside the wheelchair, pushing it through the bustling lobby, his shoulders squared but his eyes shadowed. Judy carried the bag of medications, vials and syringes rattling softly inside, the new weight of their lives.

Outside, the city bustled as though nothing had changed. Taxis honked. Vendors called. Sunlight glared off glass towers.

But for Judy and Jim, the world had tilted. They wheeled their son into the bright Boston afternoon, blind yet alive, fragile yet resilient, and knew nothing would ever be the same again.

Chapter 9

The winter wind off the Charles River had a way of slicing straight through the heaviest wool coat, carrying with it the faint tang of salt and smoke from the harbor. On certain mornings, when the sun hit just right, Judy could see the dome of MIT glinting across the water, a constant reminder that they were living at the edge of discovery, in a city where science and history walked hand in hand. For all its brick and granite, Boston had become the backdrop for a drama far more intimate and fragile than its grand avenues suggested.

Jimmie was only three years old, and already his body carried a secret most men would never fathom. The pituitary gland, the tiny master of growth, balance, and strength, was gone, destroyed during the surgery that had saved his life. He was alive, yes, miraculously so, but alive in a body that threatened to betray him, a body that without intervention might remain forever small, stunted, fragile.

The doctors had saved him once, wielding the scalpel with precision that bordered on divine. But the story did not end with survival. Now came the long fight to live, to grow, to stretch out against the cruel arithmetic of biology.

It was Dr. John Crawford who stepped into that role. He was a man of calm authority, his eyes both kind and sharp behind round spectacles. As Chief of the Pediatric Endocrine Unit at Mass General, he had seen the devastation that growth failure could bring. But he was also a pioneer, one of the first in the world to chart a path out of that shadow.

"This program," Dr. Crawford said one morning, his voice steady but not without weight, "is still experimental. We are learning as we go. But your son…" he paused, looking from Jim to Judy, "your son has a chance. A real one."

The chance came in the form of a small vial, its label handwritten in precise medical script, the contents a pale, dried powder that seemed too ordinary to carry so much hope. Human Growth Hormone. HGH. Extracted, they were told, from pituitaries, though the source was left tactfully vague. Jim suspected, with a quiet shiver he never admitted aloud, that it came from cadavers. He remembered standing at the window of their Woburn apartment one evening, the vial in his hand, staring at the powder and thinking: *This came from someone who once lived, who once walked and laughed, who once had a mother too.*

The process was as meticulous as it was terrifying. The powder had to be diluted with sterile water, the clear liquid drawn up into a needle, air bubbles tapped away with the precision of a surgeon. Dr. Crawford had insisted Jim be the one to administer the injections.

"Parents are often the best at this," he explained. "Children trust them. And it will matter, in ways you may not see now."

The first time Jim held the syringe, his hand trembled. Judy stood nearby, her eyes wide, her fingers laced tightly together. Jimmie, oblivious, squirmed on the bed, clutching Helmut the cat by the tail until the animal darted away with a yowl.

Jim knelt beside his son, heart hammering.

"Buddy," he whispered, "this might sting a little. But it's going to help you grow. Okay?"

Jimmie looked at him with the unfiltered trust only a child could hold. "Like Daddy?" he asked.

Jim swallowed hard. "Yes. Like Daddy."

The needle pierced the small thigh, and Jimmie whimpered but did not cry. Judy let out a breath she hadn't realized she was holding. Jim withdrew the syringe, capped it, and for a long moment simply held his boy in his arms. The enormity of it washed over him, how something so tiny, so fragile, could hold the weight of a future.

Week after week, the ritual continued. Jim mixed, measured, injected. Jimmie adapted quickly, sometimes making a face, sometimes squirming, but more often than not accepting the routine with stoic bravery that humbled his parents. After each injection, Judy would kiss his cheek, whispering, "That's my strong boy," as if her words could build him taller, stronger, whole.

Every few weeks they returned to Mass General, where Dr. Crawford and his team charted Jimmie's progress with almost ceremonial care. Height was recorded, blood drawn, hormones tested. The doctors were kind, but the air of scientific curiosity never quite left the room. Judy sometimes resented that, resented that her son was both patient and subject, beloved child and medical case study. But she also knew, deep down, that without these men, her boy's future might already have been written in stone.

Life, however, had a way of reminding them that hope could not erase fear.

One morning, long after Jim had left for work in Fall River, a three-hour drive away, Judy noticed something strange. Jimmie was sitting on the floor, playing with blocks, when suddenly he slumped to the side, his small body gone limp. His lips parted, and his eyes fluttered shut.

"Jimmie!" Judy cried, dropping to her knees. She shook him gently, panic clawing at her chest. For a terrifying moment, there was no response. Then, faintly, he stirred, but his skin was clammy, his breathing shallow.

Her hands trembling, Judy reached for the phone. There was only one person she trusted to act faster than panic itself: Bill Palm.

"Bill…it's Jimmie," she gasped into the receiver. "Something's wrong… he's unconscious… please…"

Bill didn't waste a second. "Stay calm, Judy. I'm coming right now. Pack a bag for the hospital."

Within minutes, his car pulled up outside, and he was at the door, coat still unbuttoned, his face drawn but determined. He lifted Jimmie into his arms as though the boy were his own grandson. "We're going to Mass General," he said firmly. "I'll drive. You sit with him."

The ride blurred past Judy's eyes, a rush of traffic and sirens in her mind, though none sounded in reality. At the hospital, doctors swarmed, questions flying faster than she could answer them. They stabilized Jimmie quickly, thank God, but the scare lingered like smoke after a fire.

Hours later, Jim arrived, his face pale, eyes hollow with fear and guilt. He strode into the ward, searching, until he found Judy in the waiting room. Without a word, she rose, and they clung to each other.

"I should have been here," Jim whispered hoarsely.

"There was nothing you could do," Judy murmured. But her voice cracked all the same.

Bill Palm was there too, his steady presence a pillar against the storm. He stayed long into the night, checking on them, speaking with doctors, even bringing Judy a cup of coffee she couldn't bring herself to drink. To him, this was not obligation but friendship of the truest kind, the kind that bore the weight of another family's fear without hesitation.

In the quiet days that followed, Bill made a suggestion to Jim that carried both compassion and finality.

"You're doing a fine job here, Jim," he said gently, one evening in the office. "Better than fine. But…" He hesitated, choosing his words with care. "This…everything your boy is going through… it's too much to shoulder without family close by. You and Judy need support. Real support. If I recommend to Union Special that you be transferred back to Chicago, near your parents, near Judy's folks… would you take it?"

Jim stared at him, torn. He had worked so hard to prove himself in Boston, to rise in the company, to honor the chance he'd been given. But in the shadow of his son's illness, career seemed suddenly small.

He swallowed hard. "If it means Jimmie gets the care he needs, and Judy isn't alone…" His voice faltered. "Then yes. Yes, we'd take it."

Bill placed a hand on his shoulder. "Then that's what we'll do."

Chapter 10

They were naturally happy to be heading back. Chicago was not just a city of smoke and steel to them; it was home, a place whose skyline had once held the shape of their childhoods. Boston had given them miracles and terror in equal measure, but now the family longed for the familiar heartbeat of Illinois.

The train of visits had been steady during their years in Massachusetts. Parents, siblings, cousins making the trek east to check on them, to see Jimmie, to marvel that the boy was still alive. Yet none of it was the same as returning to one's own soil. Chicago meant roots, meant family who could be called at a moment's notice, meant streets whose names were etched into memory rather than scribbled on maps.

But coming home was not as simple as dropping suitcases on a floor and claiming it as theirs. They had decisions to make, decisions that carried the weight of Jimmie's future. And it was Judy, always Judy, who would not let those decisions rest until they had been sharpened to clarity.

One evening, while Jimmie lay asleep in his crib in the temporary Woburn apartment they would soon leave behind, Judy spread out a collection of pamphlets and notes across the dining table. The lamplight caught the determined set of her jaw as she tapped a pencil against the edge of her notebook.

"There are two," she announced, as though reading a verdict. "Two districts. That's it. If we want Jimmie to have the right start, these are our choices."

Jim leaned back, arms folded, exhaustion carved into the lines of his face. "Two districts?"

"Yes," Judy said, sliding one pamphlet toward him. "Wheeling, northwest of the city. Or Worth, southwest. Both have resource rooms."

Jim picked up the paper, skimming, though his mind was sluggish with the weight of the day. "Resource rooms," he muttered. "Explain again."

Her eyes softened, but only slightly. She was used to explaining. "It's one location in the district, a single school, that's equipped to handle children like Jimmie. They have Braille, they have mobility training. But he's still mainstreamed with sighted kids in the regular classroom. He learns alongside them. That's the point… he doesn't grow up isolated."

Jim rubbed the back of his neck. "So he's with the other kids… but he has help when he needs it."

"Exactly," Judy said. Her voice trembled just a fraction, but she pushed on. "Jim, he's already been through so much. He deserves to have the chance to sit with his peers, to laugh with them, to be treated as if he belongs. Because he does belong."

The silence stretched. Outside, the faint sound of a car passed on the street, headlights brushing across the blinds. Jim reached for her hand at last. "Then Worth. We go to Worth."

Her eyebrows arched, surprised. "Just like that?"

He smiled faintly. "You're the teacher. I trust you."

And so it was decided. Worth. Southwest. Not Wheeling, where his own parents lived, but closer to Judy's side of the family. Six of her kin lived on the south side, parents, grandparents, an aunt, an uncle, versus his two still surviving on the north. It made sense. Family meant help, meant someone to call when the earth tilted sideways again.

Jim called his mother the next day. She was quiet on the phone, disappointed, but she understood. *Do what's best for the boy,* she said finally, though her voice carried the weight of resignation.

***

They arrived in Chicago, the city unfolding before them in a patchwork of wet streets, glistening sidewalks, and the restless hum of traffic. The moving truck rattled down narrow lanes lined with greening elms, boxes piled high inside like precarious towers of all they owned. Jimmie sat wedged between Judy and Jim in the car that followed, his small hands wrapped tightly around a stuffed dog, its fur worn thin from years of being carried everywhere. To him, it was more than a toy. It was a passport, a talisman into this new chapter of his life.

The city greeted them in its usual way: not with spectacle, but with subtler intimacies. The air smelled of rain on pavement, sharp and metallic, mixing with the faint aroma of hot dogs from a street vendor at the corner. A distant train rumbled along its tracks, the vibrations threading invisibly through neighborhoods, a reminder that in Chicago, the steel veins of the city were always in motion. Above them, the skyline jagged into the clouds, but down here, on the smaller streets, it was the rhythm of neighbors sweeping porches, children racing bicycles, and dogs barking at fences that marked the return to something like home.

Their apartment, when they arrived, was modest but practical. A three-story walk-up tucked onto a side street, with flaking white paint and a narrow stoop that sloped slightly forward, as though the building itself had grown tired from standing too long. Inside, the walls bore cracked plaster and the faint odor of old radiator heat, a scent both uninviting and oddly comforting in its familiarity. The floors creaked underfoot, and the windows rattled with each passing truck. Yet Judy saw more than the cracks and wear. From the corner of the block, she could see Worthwoods Grammar School, the very building where the resource room was housed. Its red-brick facade stood solid and unyielding, the kind of architecture built to endure generations. To Judy, it was not just a school; it was a fortress, a promise that Jimmie would not be left behind.

Standing at the window, Judy pressed her hand against the cool glass, her gaze fixed on that brick building. Proximity mattered. It felt like armor. If she could see the school, she could almost convince herself she could guard Jimmie's future by sheer willpower.

"We'll rent for now," Jim said, breaking the silence as he set down a box labeled *Kitchen*. He surveyed the apartment with a practical eye, taking in the sagging plaster, the uneven trim, the faint watermark staining the ceiling. He spoke with a careful steadiness, the kind that tried to turn compromise into reassurance. "When we find something near the school, something we can actually afford and like… we'll buy. This is just a step."

Judy turned toward him, her lips pressing together in a thoughtful line. For her, the apartment's imperfections didn't matter. The sight of that school just beyond the corner was enough. Jimmie's path would not be long bus rides into unfamiliar neighborhoods or being tucked away in an institution. No, he would walk to class each morning with the other children, breathe the same air, share the same sidewalks. That, to her, was priceless.

Jimmie, unaware of the gravity hanging in his parents' voices, sat cross-legged on the hardwood floor, his stuffed dog perched on his lap. He tilted his head toward the sound of the radiator clanking to life and giggled, amused by the metallic rhythm echoing through the apartment. "It sounds like a drum," he said, tapping his hands against the toy. His innocence broke the tension, and for a moment, both parents smiled.

"It'll do," Judy whispered finally, more to herself than to Jim. "For now, it'll do."

And so the apartment became their first foothold in Chicago, a space not chosen for beauty or comfort, but for its nearness to the place that would shape their son's days. It was less a home than a declaration: here, in the shadow of Worthwoods, they would plant themselves until the right soil appeared.

***

Life began to take on a rhythm, though it was never free of tension. Judy found herself rising early, slipping into the role of both mother and silent strategist. She read everything she could on blindness, on education, on how to prepare a child for a world that would not bend for him. Sometimes, late at night, she would sit at the small kitchen table, scribbling in a notebook while Jim snored softly in the other room. She wrote questions for teachers, strategies for Braille, notes about mobility training.

Jim carried a different burden. His days were consumed by work, by the pressure of proving himself anew in the Chicago office. But in the quiet moments, he stared at his son, small, blind, vulnerable, and felt an ache he could not name. He had injected Jimmie with growth hormone, had driven him to hospitals, had held him through seizures and unconscious spells, and still he wondered: would it ever be enough?

One evening, when the summer heat pressed thick against the windows, Jim found Judy sitting on the stoop outside, her shoulders slumped.

"What's wrong?" he asked gently.

She looked up at him, tears glistening. "I just keep thinking about the first day of school. How is he going to walk into that classroom? How will the other children treat him? What if… what if he's alone?"

Jim sank beside her, silent for a long while. Then he took her hand. "Then we'll teach him not to be afraid of alone. And we'll fight for him until he isn't."

She leaned against him, comforted not by the words themselves but by the steadiness in his voice.

***

The term "resource room" soon became part of their household vocabulary, a phrase spoken with reverence and dread all at once. Judy explained it to neighbors, to relatives, to anyone who asked.

"It's where he'll learn Braille," she would say. "Where he'll practice mobility… learning to use a cane, to navigate. But the rest of the time he'll be with the other kids. Mainstreamed."

Some nodded with polite smiles, but others looked doubtful. "Isn't that… too much?" one neighbor asked once, lowering her voice as if Jimmie could not hear. "I mean, wouldn't he be better in a special school? With children like him?"

Judy's back stiffened. "No," she said sharply. "He belongs with children his age. He belongs where he can learn to live in the real world, not apart from it."

The neighbor had flushed, muttering something about meaning no offense. But Judy did not apologize. She refused to apologize for wanting her son to stand where other children stood, even if he had to learn to do it differently.

***

Jimmie himself was blissfully unaware of the storm of plans swirling around him. At three, his world was smaller, simpler: the feel of sunlight on his skin, the sound of his mother's voice, the jingle of keys his father carried, the warmth of Helmut the cat curling at his side.

But already he was curious, reaching out with small hands, mapping his environment with touch and sound. Judy watched him, heart swelling and breaking all at once, as he traced the edges of furniture, memorizing them like braille before braille.

One afternoon, she took him by the hand and led him to the schoolyard. The building loomed tall, the playground empty in the summer heat. She placed his hand against the rough brick wall.

"This will be your school someday, sweetheart," she whispered.

Jimmie tilted his head, listening. "School?"

"Yes," Judy said softly. "A place where you'll learn. Where you'll play with other children."

He smiled faintly, though he could not see the walls or the swings. He felt only her hand in his, and for him, that was enough.

Still, Judy lay awake many nights, imagining the battles to come. Teachers who might underestimate him. Children who might mock him. Administrators who might dismiss him. She knew the world did not bend easily for the vulnerable. And yet she was determined: if she had to bend it herself, she would.

Jim, too, wrestled with unspoken fears. Sometimes he dreamed of Jimmie walking into traffic, unable to see. Other times he imagined him sitting alone in a cafeteria while laughter rang out around him. He woke drenched in sweat, staring at the ceiling, helpless.

But in the daylight, he forced optimism into his voice. "He'll be fine," he told Judy, over and over, like a mantra. "He'll be fine."

The months slipped by. They settled into the apartment, into their roles, into the fragile normalcy of preparing for a future that still felt precarious. Jim's parents drove down from the north side often, bringing food, bringing comfort, though always with a hint of sadness that the family had chosen the south. Judy's relatives came too, more numerous, their presence a steady reassurance.

Thanksgiving that year was crowded and warm, Jimmie passed from lap to lap, kissed on the forehead by grandparents who whispered prayers into his hair. Jim stood back, watching, his throat tight. This…this closeness, this support, was why they had chosen Worth. Not just for the school. For this.

That night, after everyone had gone, Jim carried Jimmie to bed. He paused at the doorway, watching his son breathe in the moonlight. A fragile boy, yes. But also a fighter, a survivor. And Jim knew, with a certainty that steadied him, that they had made the right choice.

They were home. At last.

Chapter 11

Coming back to Chicago brought a strange mix of relief and uncertainty. On one hand, home was familiar, the accents, the neighborhoods, the streets where memory itself seemed to live. On the other hand, the weight of responsibility loomed heavier than ever. Every decision we made, every mile we moved, every doctor we consulted now revolved around one small figure: Jimmie.

Boston had given us the gift of possibility. At Massachusetts General, under the sharp eyes of Dr. John Crawford, we had entered a world of science and hope that only a few families in the world could even imagine. Jimmie, without a pituitary gland, should not have been growing at all. And yet, with the miracle of human growth hormone, he had already begun to push beyond the cruel limitations that nature had set upon him. The thought of leaving Boston had been terrifying. But life cannot be lived in the waiting rooms of hospitals. Life, with all its complexity, had pulled us back west, back to Chicago, back to the tug of extended family, jobs, and something resembling normalcy.

Still, the promise of growth could not be left behind. We could not afford to let geography become the enemy of Jimmie's future.

The problem was simple but enormous: the program that Dr. Crawford ran at Mass General was highly exclusive. Parents across the country would have given anything to have their child admitted. And now here we were, two ordinary parents from Chicago, daring to ask for something extraordinary. Could the program be continued from afar? Could the hope of HGH travel with us across states, carried not by the hands of the doctor himself but through a collaboration, a trust, a bridge between medical giants?

We arranged one last visit with Dr. Crawford before leaving Boston, the kind of meeting that seemed both professional and deeply personal. He was not a man prone to sentimentality, his world was data, measurements, charts, the steady pursuit of knowledge. But there was something about Jimmie, about the tiny boy with the soft laugh and determined eyes, that seemed to disarm even the sternest of physicians.

"We will have to monitor him closely," Dr. Crawford said, his tone clipped but not unkind. "Every month. Height, weight, blood panels. No skipping."

Jim, who had learned by now to translate medical gravity into parental action, leaned forward. "Doctor, with respect, we can't be flying out here every month. That's a ticket. That's time away from work. We'd do it if we had no choice, but surely… surely, there's a way to continue the program in Chicago."

For a moment, Dr. Crawford's eyes narrowed. It was not defiance, but calculation. "This program," he reminded us, "is not just treatment. It is research. Every measurement matters. Every injection, every charting of his growth, it all contributes to the science. You're asking me to extend that trust to someone else."

"And we're asking," Judy said softly but firmly, "because we have no choice."

There was silence then, the kind that stretches like a taut rope across a canyon. Finally, Crawford scribbled a name onto his notepad and tore the paper away. "Dr. Steiner. Pediatric endocrinology. Chicago. If he is willing, and if he applies to participate, perhaps we can arrange it."

It felt like a door cracking open in a storm.

***

The drive to meet Dr. Steiner felt endless, one of those Chicago trips that made the city seem less like a single place and more like a sprawling universe stitched together by congested arteries. Thirty-five miles may as well have been a hundred. The traffic snarled, horns blared, and every stoplight seemed to linger just a shade too long. Jim gripped the wheel, eyes fixed on the road, while Judy sat beside him, quiet but taut with worry.

In the backseat, Jimmie hummed tunelessly to himself, tapping his little shoes against the seat, blissfully unaware of the storm his parents carried in their chests. To him, this was just another car ride, another day with Mommy and Daddy. To them, it was everything.

"Do you think he'll agree?" Judy asked finally, her voice breaking the silence.

Jim kept his eyes forward. "He has to."

"What if he doesn't?"

"Then I'll drive to Boston every month if I have to. But he will." Jim's voice was flat, steel pressed thin by exhaustion. "He has to."

When they finally pulled into the hospital parking lot, the building loomed like a fortress of glass and stone. Inside, the waiting room smelled faintly of antiseptic, sharp and sterile, as if to remind everyone who entered that this was a place where science ruled. The flicker of a wall-mounted television cast cartoon colors across the linoleum floor. Jimmie wriggled on Jim's knee, legs swinging, laughing at something only he found funny.

Judy smoothed the boy's hair, her hand lingering as if the touch could ward off whatever news lay ahead. Jim tried to steady his breathing. He hated hospitals, hated the waiting, hated the way each second seemed stretched by unseen hands into something unbearable.

Then the door opened.

Dr. Steiner entered with a brisk step, younger than Dr. Crawford, his face softer, his presence less intimidating. He smiled immediately, not the professional politeness of a man fulfilling a duty, but the kind of smile that reached the eyes.

"And this must be Jimmie," he said, kneeling down so he was eye level with the boy.

Jimmie tilted his head, curious. "Are you the new doctor?"

"That's right," Steiner said gently. "I'm Dr. Steiner. And I'm here to help."

Something eased in Judy's shoulders. It wasn't much, but enough that she breathed a little easier.

Steiner stood and extended his hand to Jim. "I've heard about the program. Dr. Crawford's work has been groundbreaking. To see a child like Jimmie as part of it… well, it's extraordinary."

Jim gripped the doctor's hand tightly, as though trying to transfer some of his own resolve. "We're just hoping it can continue. We can't manage Boston every month. We need you."

Steiner studied them, then glanced back at Jimmie, who had now discovered a stack of children's books and was flipping them upside down, pretending to read.

"I will contact Dr. Crawford," Steiner said at last. "If he approves, I would be honored to participate. This kind of continuity is rare in medicine, and Jimmie deserves nothing less."

The words landed like an anchor dropped into turbulent seas. Judy closed her eyes for a moment, her hand finding Jim's. They had not been dismissed, not brushed aside, not lost in the shuffle of bureaucracy.

For the first time in weeks, there was hope that didn't feel fragile.

***

The weeks that followed stretched like wire pulled taut. Every day they checked the mailbox. Every phone call set Judy's heart pounding. They lived in the suspense of bureaucracy, where decisions that could change a child's life moved at the speed of paper.

Jimmie, of course, knew nothing of it. He played, he laughed, he grew restless, all the while blissfully untroubled by the battle waged in his name. His innocence was a mercy and a torment both.

Finally, the letter arrived. Arrangements had been made. Approval had been given. Jimmie's monthly visits would shift from Boston to Chicago. The program would continue.

The vials still arrived, sealed tight, small enough to hold in a hand yet carrying the weight of destiny. Each one was precious, as if every bottle contained not just medicine but possibility itself.

At the kitchen table, Jim performed the ritual. He laid out the syringe, steadying his hands though his heart thundered. Judy hovered nearby, the silence in the room deep enough to hear the clock ticking. Jimmie sat patiently, though his eyes narrowed with suspicion.

"Daddy, is it gonna hurt?" he asked in that small, uncertain voice.

Jim forced a smile. "Just a pinch, buddy. Like a mosquito bite. But this one makes you stronger."

"Stronger than Joey's dog?" Jimmie asked, remembering the neighbor's bounding Labrador.

"Stronger than anything," Jim answered, though his throat caught on the words.

The needle slid in, a quick prick, a gasp, and then it was over. Jimmie scowled at first, then laughed, as if eager to prove that pain could not claim him.

Every injection felt like touching fate with a needle. Every inch Jimmie grew was a defiance, a declaration that he would not be defined by what was missing inside his body.

And with each passing month, as the tape measure confirmed what love already knew, Jim and Judy clung to the hope that their boy's future, which was fragile, precious, hard-won, was slowly, steadily, being built.

***

If medicine gave them hope, Worthwoods gave them belonging.

The neighborhood itself seemed almost conjured from another time, tucked away as if the world had forgotten it. Three blocks by six, hemmed in by ancient oaks whose branches arched overhead like cathedral ceilings. In summer, their leaves rustled like whispered prayers; in autumn, they burned with gold and scarlet fire. The streets were narrow and old-fashioned, crowned in the middle, sloping gently to shallow ditches that carried away the rain. After a storm, the water pooled there, turning the neighborhood into a mirror world where trees doubled themselves in shimmering reflections, as if to remind residents they lived inside something rare, almost enchanted.

Every evening, Jim found himself driving slowly through those streets, circling like a moth drawn to light. Jimmie rode in the backseat, nose pressed to the glass, narrating every dog he saw, every bicycle that whizzed past, every flicker of porchlight. Judy sat beside Jim, her hand often resting against her chin, half amused, half weary of his ritual.

"You're obsessed," she said one night, her tone gentle, carrying more affection than scolding.

Jim didn't look at her. His eyes stayed forward, scanning the porches, the yards, the faint glow of living room windows. "I'm not looking for just a house," he said. His voice was steady, deliberate, as though the words had been rehearsed. "I'm looking for the house. For him. For Jimmie."

Judy exhaled, her breath fogging slightly against the window. "And what if we never find it?"

The silence that followed seemed to hang between them like a fragile thread. Then Jim's hand tightened on the wheel. "We will." His conviction was not loud, but it had weight, like iron laid down on a table.

The search continued. Weeks of circling, driving, hoping. Some nights Jim slowed in front of homes with neat gardens and white shutters, only to shake his head. Too polished. Too cold. Other times Judy pointed at larger houses with sprawling lawns, but Jim's answer was always the same: "That's not it."

And then one afternoon, as if placed directly in their path, they saw it.

It was nothing grand, nothing a passerby might stop to marvel at. A modest home, small but inviting, set back from the road as though it wanted to be discovered, not flaunted. In the yard leaned a hand-painted sign, crooked on its post, the red letters reading simply: **For Sale.**

Jim pulled over, the car crunching against the gravel at the curb. For a long moment, they said nothing, just stared. The house was quiet, worn at the edges, but there was a warmth to it, as though it had been waiting for them all along. Two bedrooms. A large kitchen. A living room with a fireplace that seemed less like brick and mortar and more like a promise of nights gathered together, safe from whatever the world hurled outside.

Behind the house stretched nearly half an acre of land, untamed and generous, wildflowers spilling along the edges in bursts of color. It was not manicured; it was not perfect. But it was alive, breathing, as though it had kept its soul intact while other houses around it had traded theirs for polish.

Judy's hand shot to Jim's arm, clutching it as if to steady herself. Her voice trembled. "This is it."

From the backseat came a small gasp, followed by the scrabbling sound of little hands pressing against the glass. Jimmie's eyes were wide as though he could see. "Does it have a tree I can climb?" he asked breathlessly, hope cracking through his voice.

Jim leaned back, his lips curving into a grin. He didn't even have to look, he had already seen it, the great oak standing sentinel near the fence line, its branches strong and sprawling like arms wide open.

"It's got a whole forest, son," he said.

And in that moment, the house was no longer just lumber and walls. It was sanctuary. It was belonging. It was the soil where hope could take root and grow.

***

Moving in felt like planting roots in soil they hadn't realized they'd been searching for. The fireplace quickly became the center of family life, evenings gathered in front of it, Judy reading aloud while Jimmie nestled against her, Jim stoking the flames as though each spark could keep their fragile world alight.

Neighbors stopped by with casseroles and handshakes. Some knew about Jimmie's condition; others only saw a cheerful boy with a quick laugh. But everywhere there was kindness, and everywhere the sense that this place, this wooded rectangle of streets, had been waiting for them.

And yet, even in Worthwoods, Jim sometimes lay awake, staring at the ceiling, thinking about the injections. About the cadaver-derived hormone, about the risks no one fully understood, about the fact that he, not a doctor, was the one pushing the needle into his child's flesh.

Judy would sense the tension beside her. "You're doing everything you can," she whispered in the dark.

"I just don't want to fail him," Jim admitted.

"You won't," she said, her hand finding his. "You can't."

Every choice, be it the program, the doctor, the house, the neighborhood, circled back to one truth: Jimmie. His chance at growth. His chance at independence. His chance at a life where blindness and stature were challenges, not prisons.

The house wasn't just a house. It was a promise. The neighborhood wasn't just trees and roads. It was freedom. And every injection, every appointment, every late-night worry was part of the same unspoken vow: he would have a future.

And so, in Worthwoods, under the shade of oaks and the watchful eye of science, their lives pressed forward: fragile, determined, luminous with hope.

Chapter 12

The new house felt like sunlight breaking through after a long winter. They had waited, searched, driven circles through Worthwoods until the streets themselves seemed worn into Jim's mind. And now, here it was: theirs.

Jimmie ran first, small legs pumping, laughter spilling into the quiet yard as though he wanted the house to hear him, to know it had a child waiting to fill its walls with noise. He bolted through the front door, sneakers squeaking on the wooden floor, and vanished into the rooms with a shout of discovery.

"Mine!" he called from somewhere down the hallway. "This one's mine!"

Jim and Judy followed, stepping into the living room that smelled faintly of plaster and fresh paint. The fireplace stood proudly in the corner, its brick mantle broad and solid. Judy traced a finger along it, imagining stockings at Christmas, late-night fires crackling while Jimmie fell asleep on the rug.

"He already picked his room," Jim said with a laugh, setting down the first of many cardboard boxes.

"I can hear," Judy answered, listening to Jimmie's excited footsteps pounding across the floor. Her face softened. "It feels right, doesn't it? Like it was waiting for us."

Jim turned in a slow circle, eyes taking in the brickwork, the clean lines of the walls, the smell of wood polish. "Yeah," he said. "It feels solid. Like it'll hold."

***

Jimmie's new bedroom became his kingdom. The double-decker bunk beds had been Judy's idea, insisting that someday Jimmie would want friends to stay over. When the delivery men brought them in, Jimmie couldn't *see* the bunk beds, but his hands moved eagerly over the smooth wood. Judy smiled and said softly, "Here are your bunk beds," and Jimmie's eyes grew as wide as the moon.

"Two beds?" he asked in awe.

"One for you," Judy said, smoothing the blanket across the lower bunk. "And one for whoever you invite to sleep over."

"Or both for me!" Jimmie shouted, immediately climbing the ladder. He scrambled onto the top bunk and flopped onto his stomach, legs kicking like he had just conquered Everest. "I can sleep up here one night, down there the next night, then up again. It's like… like two rooms in one!"

Judy laughed and Jim leaned against the doorframe, arms folded, watching his son with quiet pride. "Looks like he doesn't miss the old apartment."

"Not one bit," Judy murmured, her eyes misting just slightly.

On the dresser, Jimmie placed his red toy fire truck, positioning it carefully so the ladder pointed toward the window. "This is the station," he announced. "If there's ever a fire, they can come down the bunk and out the window!"

"Good plan," Jim said with mock seriousness. "You'll have the safest room in the neighborhood."

***

If Jimmie claimed the bedroom, Judy claimed the kitchen. For years she had wrestled with small galley kitchens in cramped apartments, where counter space was scarce and every meal felt like a puzzle of juggling pots and pans.

Here, light spilled through a wide window over the sink, falling across gleaming new appliances, a stove that shone, a refrigerator big enough to actually hold leftovers, counters that stretched like promises.

On the first morning, she brewed coffee while Jim read the paper at the kitchen table. Jimmie clattered his spoon against his cereal bowl, humming some tuneless melody. Judy turned slowly in the middle of the kitchen, almost overwhelmed by the space.

"I could cook Thanksgiving dinner in here," she said aloud.

Jim peered over the paper. "You already do."

"Yes, but in this kitchen I could do it without swearing." She leaned against the counter, eyes shining. "I feel like I can breathe in here, Jim."

He folded the paper, stood, and kissed the top of her head. "Good. You deserve to."

***

For Jim, it wasn't the kitchen or even the cozy living room that hooked him. It was the face brick running all the way around the house, and the two-car garage with its wide, yawning door. He opened it that first weekend and stood with his hands on his hips, breathing in the cool concrete smell, already envisioning the workbench he would build.

"This," he said, sweeping his hand as though introducing a masterpiece, "is where I'll fix everything you break."

Judy arched an eyebrow. "Oh, you mean everything you break."

Jimmie darted in, his toy truck clutched in one hand. "Can I fix things too, Daddy?"

Jim crouched down, ruffling his son's hair. "One day. I'll build a bench right here, and you can have a stool next to mine."

Jimmie's face lit up, and for a fleeting moment Jim saw the future: father and son, side by side, tools scattered, laughter echoing in the garage. It wasn't just a garage. It was a place where a boy could learn from his father, where time could stretch long enough to leave memories behind.

Even though the house was larger than anything they had lived in before, Jimmie moved through it as though it had always been his. He never seemed lost, never clung nervously to Judy's hand. He knew the layout quickly, tracing walls with his fingers, counting steps from one room to another. The fireplace, the kitchen table, the back door, all became familiar anchors.

And beyond their front yard, the neighborhood opened its arms.

The Goys across the street had the biggest house on the block and, more importantly in Jimmie's eyes, a big swimming pool. Summer weekends meant music drifting across the road, the splash of children, the smell of charcoal smoke from the grill. The Goys invited neighbors regularly, and it wasn't long before Judy found herself in conversation with Mrs. Goy about schools and recipes, while Jimmie dangled his legs in the pool alongside their two children, who were a little older but patient with him.

Two doors down lived the Larsons. Their son Todd was Jimmie's age: bright-haired, mischievous, with the kind of energy that turned sidewalks into racetracks. The first time they met, Todd had been riding his bike in endless circles. He braked suddenly, dust skidding beneath his tires, and called, "Hey! You wanna play?"

Jimmie hesitated, tilting his head toward the sound. "What are you playing?"

"Anything," Todd said with a grin. "We can play tag, or war, or pretend we're explorers."

From then on, the two were inseparable.

Next door lived the Akikadious family, with a younger girl who followed the older children like a shadow. Jimmie treated her kindly, though sometimes with the exasperation of an older brother. Judy liked knowing the neighborhood had a balance, older kids to look up to, younger ones to teach.

***

When fall came, the sidewalks filled each morning with children heading to Worthwoods School. Jimmie walked with Todd and the others, his cane tapping lightly, his steps confident.

At school, Todd was in all the same classes except for the times Jimmie slipped away to the resource room. There, he learned Braille, running his small fingers over the raised dots, struggling some days, triumphing on others. He practiced mobility skills, counting steps, learning to navigate spaces without fear.

Some of the other students in the resource room came from far-off neighborhoods, bussed in for their lessons. They didn't know the children Jimmie spent recess with; they scattered back to their buses at the end of the day. But Jimmie ate lunch with Todd, played kickball with the others, and at the end of the day walked home with his friends. He wasn't an outsider here. He was part of the fabric.

One afternoon, Judy asked him as he slid into his chair for supper, "Did you feel left out today, when you went to the resource room?"

Jimmie shook his head, grinning as he shoveled mashed potatoes onto his fork. "Nope. Todd waited for me after. And at lunch, we traded cookies. He gave me a chocolate chip."

Jim caught Judy's eyes across the table. Relief softened the tightness in her chest. He was not just surviving; he was belonging.

The house became more than a shelter. It became memory, ritual, laughter echoing through rooms at night. It became Judy's haven, Jim's pride, and Jimmie's kingdom.

Worthwoods had welcomed them, folded them in. And though challenges still lay ahead: tests, doctor's visits, questions about the future, in those first months, the weight lifted.

For the first time in years, they weren't just surviving. They were living.

Chapter 13

The house had barely settled around them before Judy's restless energy returned. For years she had devoted herself to Jimmie's care, her days shaped around doctor's appointments, new therapies, hospital corridors, and the endless vigilance of a mother watching her son navigate a fragile path. But now, in the quiet of Worthwoods, with Jimmie walking confidently to school each morning and returning in the afternoons with stories tumbling out of his mouth, Judy felt the itch of her old profession stir again.

"Maybe," she said one evening, stirring spaghetti sauce in her new kitchen, "it's time I went back to teaching."

Jim looked up from the evening paper, the smell of garlic and simmering tomatoes filling the room. "You've been saying that more and more lately."

"Because I can't stop thinking about it." She set the spoon down and faced him fully, her eyes bright but edged with uncertainty. "The timing feels right. Jimmie is settled. The school has resource rooms, the teachers know him, the neighborhood feels safe. And…" She hesitated, then smiled. "I miss it. I miss the classroom. The kids. The noise. Even the homework piles."

Jim folded the paper and leaned back, studying her. "We could use the money."

"That's not why," Judy said quickly. "I want my income to go into savings. Or maybe for special things… trips, experiences, things Jimmie will remember. But mostly… I want to feel like myself again."

There was a silence between them, broken only by Jimmie's voice drifting from the living room where he hummed to himself, lining up his toy trucks in perfect rows.

"You'd still be home when he's home," Jim said slowly. "Summers, winters, holidays…"

"Exactly. Same schedule. Same rhythm."

Jim's lips curved into a smile. "Then do it."

***

The application process was quicker than Judy expected. Perhaps it was her confidence, sharpened by years of advocating for Jimmie in hospitals and schools. Perhaps it was her reputation from her earlier years of teaching. Whatever it was, the district welcomed her back.

When the letter came confirming her position as a second-grade teacher, Judy held it in both hands as though it were a fragile relic. "It's official," she whispered, eyes wide. "I'm going back."

The morning of her first day, she smoothed her skirt three times before leaving the house, nerves fluttering in her stomach like a girl heading to her own first day of school. Jimmie, sitting at the kitchen table with his cereal, cocked his head at the sound of her fussing.

"You're nervous," he said matter-of-factly.

Judy laughed. "A little. How can you tell?"

"I can hear it," Jimmie said, spoon halfway to his mouth. "Your voice is higher. Like when you're about to yell at Dad for forgetting to take the trash out."

Jim, pouring his coffee, chuckled. "He's not wrong."

Judy kissed Jimmie's head, inhaling the familiar scent of milk and sleep. "Wish me luck."

"You don't need luck," Jimmie replied. "You're the smartest teacher."

And with that, Judy stepped back into the world she had once loved.

***

Teaching again was both a blessing and a burden. Judy thrived in the classroom, the hum of chatter, the flash of curiosity in her students' eyes, the satisfaction of guiding them through fractions and reading passages. But she also felt the pull at home. Grading papers late at night meant less time for quiet talks with Jim. Preparing lesson plans on weekends sometimes clashed with family outings.

Still, the rhythm worked. She and Jimmie shared a schedule. They walked into school together each morning, Judy carrying her tote bag heavy with books, Jimmie tapping his cane lightly on the pavement, Todd chattering beside him. In the afternoons, they left together too, Jimmie clutching his lunchbox, Judy exhausted but glowing.

One evening, Jim found her at the kitchen table surrounded by stacks of spelling tests. "Are we sure this isn't too much?" he asked gently.

Judy looked up, a pencil tucked behind her ear, her hair falling loose around her face. "It's a lot," she admitted. Then she glanced toward Jimmie's room, where their son was humming as he practiced Braille. "But it feels right. For me. For him."

***

The Worth School District had many schools, *Worthwoods* being one of them. Judy thought it best not to teach at the same school where Jimmie would be attending, so she chose to teach instead at *Worth Main School*. It felt like a wise balance, close enough to be near him, yet far enough to let him find his own rhythm.

That Christmas, Jim wheeled a new bicycle into the living room, a bright red 24-inch bike with a gleaming banana seat and chrome handlebars. Jimmie gasped, though he could not see it and didn't yet know what it was. His hands moved slowly, reverently, over the smooth metal, tracing the curves as though reading its story through touch alone.

"My bike?" he breathed.

"Your bike," Jim confirmed, pride swelling in his chest.

Jimmie wasn't quite tall enough for a full-size bike, but this one fit him just right. The streets of Worthwoods weren't paved, no curbs, no sidewalks, just crowned roads covered in loose stone, perfect for learning to ride. The crunch of gravel beneath the tires made its own music, a rhythm all his own.

On that first ride, Judy stood nearby, wringing her hands nervously at the edge of the gravel. "Are you sure this is safe?" she asked.

"Safe enough," Jim said, steadying Jimmie as he climbed on. "We'll take it slow."

Jimmie gripped the handlebars, his face set with fierce determination. "Don't hold on too long, Dad."

Jim jogged beside him, hand on the seat, heart pounding. "Okay. Ready? Pedal. Pedal steady…"

The tires crunched. The bike wobbled. And then, Jimmie was moving, really moving, his legs pumping, his back straight, the wind lifting his hair. Jim let go, breath caught in his throat.

"I'm doing it!" Jimmie shouted, joy ringing through the quiet Worthwoods street. "I'm riding!"

Judy pressed her hand to her mouth, tears springing to her eyes as neighbors peeked out from their windows, drawn by the sound of triumph.

That same winter, one Christmas later, Jim and Judy surprised him again, with something a bit bigger. In the living room, beside the wrapped presents, they placed a shiny helmet with a string attached, leading all the way out to the garage. There, waiting quietly, was a small 100cc motorcycle.

When Jimmie followed the string and felt the shape of the bike, he gasped again, part disbelief, part pure wonder. Of course, he wasn't allowed to ride it alone, but he *did* ride with his dad, sitting in front of him, Jim's steady hands at the controls… *most of the time.*

Later that January, they discovered that Todd had already seen the motorcycle in the garage before Christmas and had tipped Jimmie off. Still, that first ride together, Jimmie's laughter cutting through the cold air, was one of those moments no one ever forgot.

***

Riding with his friends, Jimmie learned quickly how to navigate. The crown of the road guided him; the subtle shift of the street told him when he veered too far. The crunch of gravel beneath his tires echoed off parked cars, letting him know where obstacles lay. What his eyes could not give him, his ears and skin supplied.

One afternoon, he burst through the front door, cheeks flushed. "I rode around the block!" he announced breathlessly.

Jim lifted him off the bike in a bear hug. "Around the whole block? That's my boy."

Jimmie grinned, chest heaving. "I stayed right in the middle. I could feel the road pulling if I went too far. And the cars… I could hear them in the stones."

Judy, though proud, couldn't help but frown. "Stones and sound are not supposed to be your traffic signals, young man."

Jimmie only shrugged, mischief in his smile. "It worked, didn't it?"

Jim's laughter broke the tension, but Judy's heart carried the weight of it long after. Her son was daring the world, blind but determined to race headlong into it.

***

From his mobility classes, Jimmie had learned another skill: to sense the movement of air. He discovered that indoors, when the air shifted, he could feel the subtle rise against his skin just before a wall or doorway. It became his compass, a quiet guide.

But more than that, he cultivated a kind of silence, a stubborn independence. He hated the cane at times, hated the idea of being marked as blind. He practiced moving without it, memorizing the house so thoroughly he could reach for every drawer, every cupboard, every doorknob without error.

Judy watched him one evening as he padded through the kitchen, opening a cabinet, fetching a cup, pouring milk without spilling a drop.

"You didn't use your cane," she said softly.

"I don't need it here," Jimmie answered, his voice steady. "I know where everything is."

Her eyes filled, torn between pride and fear. Pride in his ability, fear in the risks he insisted on taking. "Just promise me," she whispered, "that you won't pretend too much."

Jimmie set the milk down, lifting his chin. "I'm not pretending. I'm living."

And in that moment, Judy realized her son was not merely surviving blindness. He was wrestling with it, challenging it, shaping his own way through the dark.

The months unfolded with triumphs and stumbles, Judy balancing her classroom and her motherhood, Jim steady at her side, and Jimmie growing not only in inches but in courage. The house they had bought gave them stability; Judy's job gave them structure; Jimmie's determination gave them hope.

Every stone-crunching ride, every air-sensed wall, every carefully memorized drawer was more than skill. It was defiance. It was Jimmie's declaration that the world, no matter how blurred or unseen, would still belong to him.

And for his parents, it was both the greatest blessing and the heaviest burden: to watch their son carve his own path, sometimes against the very walls meant to protect him.

Chapter 14

The smell of fresh-cut balsa wood lingered in the kitchen that winter, as if the house itself had become a workshop. Jim sat at the table with Jimmie beside him, the boy's small hands tracing the smooth block that would soon become something far more than wood and wheels.

The Cub Scouts had announced their **Pinewood Derby**, and in the Worthwoods neighborhood, it was spoken about with almost the same reverence as Christmas. Boys whispered strategies at recess, mothers exchanged tips over back fences, and fathers, though they weren't supposed to build the cars, couldn't resist standing a little too long in garages, eyeing saws and sandpaper.

For Jimmie, the Derby was not just another event. It was a chance. A chance to prove he belonged.

"Feel this, Dad," Jimmie said one evening, running his fingers over the body he had been sanding for what seemed like hours. "Smooth, right? No bumps. Just like the Hot Wheels I keep on my shelf."

Jim smiled. "Smooth as glass, buddy. You've got the patience of a craftsman."

Patience was something Jimmie had in spades. Perhaps it was because of the blindness, the way his world forced him to pause, to sense, to absorb details others might miss. But here, sanding balsa wood until the grain whispered beneath his fingertips, he wasn't a boy with limits. He was a boy building a machine that would fly.

Their kitchen turned into a nightly ritual. Judy would prepare dinner, and when the dishes were cleared, Jim would set the hand drill and the emery cloth on the table. Jimmie would lean close, listening to the hum of the spinning nails, also used as the axles of the car, as his father held them steady.

Together, they polished them down until they shone like silver, smooth enough to trick friction into forgetting its purpose.

"You hear that?" Jimmie asked once, head cocked to the sound of the spinning nail. "That's speed. I can tell."

Jim chuckled, but Judy, standing at the counter, looked over with misted eyes. She saw what her son was doing, not pretending sight, but shaping vision out of sound, touch, and imagination.

They painted the body dark blue, a leftover color from the kitchen cabinets, and when the brush dried in Jimmie's hand, he whispered, "This is my dark horse. Nobody sees it coming."

Jim added one last design feature, though he never admitted it outright as his own idea. He drilled small holes into the back and filled them with **BBs** for weight, sealing them in like secret ammunition.

"This isn't cheating, right?" Jimmie asked when he heard the rattling of the BBs before they were closed inside.

"No, son," Jim replied. "It's called strategy."

***

The school gymnasium was packed the afternoon of the race. Folding chairs lined the edges, parents clutching coffee cups and cameras, boys bouncing with excitement. At the front of the room stood the track: four long wooden lanes sloping downward from a tall incline, ending in a flat finish line with a string of lights ready to flash the winner.

Jimmie clutched his car in both hands. He had memorized every curve of it, every wheel, every line of paint. To anyone else, it was just another entry in a sea of cars. To him, it was a declaration.

Todd Larson slapped him on the shoulder. "Yours looks fast, Jimmie. Bet mine beats it, though."

Jimmie grinned, tilting his head toward the sound of Todd's voice. "You'll see dust, Todd. Nothing but dust."

The laughter between them sounded like friendship, pure and easy.

When Jimmie's heat was called, Jim guided him to the track but let his son set the car himself. Jimmie crouched low, fingertips hovering over the lane until he found the groove. He placed the car carefully, like a priest setting a chalice on an altar.

"Ready?" the announcer called.

The barrier lifted.

The cars shot forward, wheels rattling against wood, the crowd roaring. Jimmie stood frozen, his hands clenched in fists at his sides, listening. He could hear it. The unique hum of his wheels, the way they spun smoother than the others. And then, the eruption of cheers.

"Winner: Lane Three!"

Jim lifted Jimmie into the air, the boy's laughter echoing off the gym walls. He had done it. His car had not just competed, it had flown.

Heat after heat, the car proved itself. Each time, Jimmie's smile grew wider, though Jim couldn't shake a small fear: that the other parents would whisper, *the father built it for him*. But as the final race ended, with Jimmie's car crossing the line nearly half a track ahead, the applause was real. No pity, no charity, just respect.

Later, as they packed up, one father leaned over and clapped Jim on the shoulder. "Your boy's got a knack. Blind or not, he built a winner."

And for the first time in a long while, Jim felt the weight lift.

***

The victory was sweet, but home was about to grow louder, softer, messier… all at once.

It began with a family friend who arrived one Sunday with a wriggling bundle of fur in her arms.

"She needs a home," the friend said. "Mostly German Shepherd, I think. Sweet as they come. Just... nobody wanted her."

The puppy was black and tan, her ears comically floppy, her eyes wide with a devotion she hadn't yet earned. Jimmie dropped to his knees on the carpet, and the pup bounded into his arms as if she had been waiting her whole life for this boy.

"She's mine," Jimmie whispered into her fur. "All mine."

They named her **Pfister**, a name chosen in *friendly retaliation* after Judy's cousin's family, the Pfisters, who owned a cow named *Valentine*. The name had a slightly German sound to it, and it stuck. It felt noble, almost commanding, though Pfister herself had far more clumsy grace than authority. She failed obedience classes spectacularly, preferring to flop into Jimmie's lap rather than heel. But what she lacked in discipline, she more than made up for in loyalty. She followed Jimmie from room to room, curled faithfully at the foot of his bed, and barked whenever strangers came near the yard.

"Not smart," Jim muttered once after Pfister failed to fetch a ball for the tenth time, "but loyal."

Judy smiled. "That's more than enough."

And to Jimmie, she was more than a dog. She was freedom. With Pfister at his side, he dared to wander further down the street, dared to play rougher with the neighborhood kids, dared to believe he wasn't fragile.

***

Pfister's arrival should have been the end of it, but Judy, ever the heart of the home, declared balance was needed.

"If we have a dog," she said, "we ought to have a cat, too."

Jimmie clapped his hands in delight. "Yes! And I know his name already. Tigger… with two Gs. Double ggrr."

They adopted a striped orange kitten from the shelter, a mischievous little creature who seemed to exist only to pounce on Pfister's tail and race through the house at midnight. Pfister tolerated him with saintly patience, often sighing deeply as Tigger batted her ears.

To Jimmie, though, Tigger was the perfect counterpoint to Pfister's steady devotion. Where Pfister was loyal and protective, Tigger was unpredictable, wild, teaching Jimmie that not every companion had to guide, some simply had to make you laugh.

***

One of Jimmie's favorite memories wasn't about grand events or milestones, it was about something as simple as sitting together in their own backyard on a golden summer evening. The Worthwoods lot was half an acre of wild beauty, a patchwork of grass and wildflowers rimmed with oaks that caught the late light in nets of gold. They'd pull out lawn chairs after dinner, Jim with a tall glass of iced tea, Judy with her knitting, and Jimmie leaning back, his face tilted toward the sun, listening.

That was when Pfister and Tigger put on their shows.

It always began the same way: Tigger crouched low, tail flicking, every muscle quivering as though he were a lion in the Serengeti instead of a striped cat in a suburban yard. Pfister would stand ten feet away, head cocked, ears bouncing like loose curtains. Then, without warning, Pfister would launch herself forward in a mad gallop.

"Here she goes!" Jim would announce, voice rich with mock drama. "The great hound of Worthwoods, charging with thunder in her paws!"

At the very last second, Tigger would leap skyward, legs stretched, missing Pfister's nose by a whisker. He landed lightly, tail high, and Pfister skidded across the grass with a puzzled yelp.

"Olé!" Jimmie would cry, clapping his hands as though watching a bullfight. He couldn't see the leap, but his father's narration painted it sharper than sight ever could: the rustle of Pfister's paws, the whistle of air as Tigger sprang, the triumphant yowl as the cat escaped yet again.

The game repeated itself until twilight. Judy would eventually gather her things and announce, "Alright, you two matadors, time for baths before bed." But for Jimmie, the memory was permanent, the warmth of the evening, his father's voice turning a pet's roughhousing into legend, the sense that the world was both safe and alive around him.

***

Summers also brought Wednesday afternoons, which held their own kind of magic. Judy had taken a teaching job in the district, and though her days were often long, she made Wednesdays sacred. She would pick Jimmie up after school and together they'd fly down the road in her Corvette, the top pulled down so the air whipped past them in wild, thrilling bursts.

"Faster, Mom, faster!" Jimmie would cry, gripping the dash, hair whipping in every direction.

Judy laughed, the sound carried away by the wind. "Don't tell your father I'm driving like this!"

To Jimmie, that ride was freedom, the sensation of the car slicing the air, the roar of the engine, the rush of possibility. By the time they pulled into **Lincolnshire Country Club**, he was flushed with excitement.

The pool became Jimmie's second classroom. At first, he was hesitant, the water vast and unknowable, but the instructors guided him patiently. They taught him to trust the rhythm of his body: kick, breathe, pull. Soon, to the astonishment of onlookers, he was slicing through the water with a crawl stroke that was precise and steady.

"Look at him go," one of the lifeguards remarked. "He's like a little torpedo."

And he was, lap after lap, arms cutting, head turning for breath at just the right moment. He swam not like a boy with limitations, but like a boy who had discovered an element where his blindness meant nothing at all. Underwater, everyone was sightless; underwater, it was sound, breath, and motion that mattered.

While Jimmie swam, Judy joined the "Nine-Holers," a group of women who played nine holes of golf each week. The clink of their clubs and their bursts of laughter drifted across the greens, a reminder that Judy, too, was carving out her joy in those afternoons. She liked knowing Jimmie was close, cared for, safe, and he liked knowing she was near, her laughter riding the breeze.

On Fridays, Jim would meet them for dinner at the club, a small ritual that knit the family tighter. The three of them would sit together, Pfister and Tigger waiting at home, the glow of belonging stretching across their table like candlelight.

But perhaps the proudest moment of that summer came not in the water or on the green, but in the echo of music.

Jimmie had discovered the drums. What began as a restless tapping on tables and countertops turned into lessons, and before long, he was playing rhythms with a confidence that startled even him. The beat became his language: measured, precise, alive.

One evening, while the family lingered at the club after dinner, a member who often played the piano noticed Jimmie keeping rhythm with his hands on the table.

"You've got a good ear, young man," he said. "How'd you like to join me for a song or two?"

Jimmie's face flushed. "Really?"

Jim and Judy exchanged a glance, both nervous and proud.

Minutes later, Jimmie was seated at the drum kit, legs barely reaching the pedals. The pianist began a jaunty tune, and Jimmie's sticks answered, filling the room with rhythm that was not perfect, but bold and alive. The crowd clapped along, the sound carrying Jimmie further into confidence.

When the last note faded, the applause rose. Jimmie grinned so wide his cheeks ached. And of course, he had insisted on wearing his white, zip-up patent leather boots… his "performing boots." To him, they were magic, the final touch that turned him from a boy into a showman.

That night, Judy whispered as she tucked him into bed, "Not bad for grammar school, my love. Not bad at all."

Jimmie fell asleep smiling, the echo of drums still thrumming in his chest.

***

By spring, the Worthwoods house felt alive in ways no apartment ever could. The walls echoed with Jimmie's laughter, the scuffle of Pfister's paws, the thud of Tigger landing on countertops he wasn't supposed to reach.

Neighbors waved more often now, stopping by with casseroles or leaning on fences to chat. The Larson boy, Todd, was a constant presence, his friendship with Jimmie growing deeper each day. Together they biked the crowned streets, their laughter carrying over the sound of crunching gravel.

And Judy, though weary from balancing teaching and motherhood, often paused in the doorway of her classroom or her kitchen to watch it all unfold, the boy, the dog, the cat, the neighborhood that had finally begun to feel like a promise kept.

Life was not simple, not easy. Jimmie still wrestled with his blindness, still tried to pretend at times that he could see. But in the dark blue of his Pinewood Derby car, in the loyal bark of Pfister, in the mischievous pounce of Tigger, he was not defined by what he lacked. He was defined by the world he was building, piece by piece, with family, love, and grit.

And in that house in Worthwoods, they all began to believe it: belonging wasn't given. It was made.

Chapter 15

Graduation from Worthwoods School was nothing short of a milestone. For Jimmie, it marked more than the end of grammar school, it was the closing of one chapter and the bold opening of another. The auditorium brimmed with family, teachers, and classmates, each of them buzzing with excitement, anticipation, and the sweet scent of carnations pinned to freshly pressed shirts and dresses.

Jimmie sat among his peers, shoulders back, a quiet confidence radiating from him. He wasn't nervous; he was ready. He had built friendships in every corner of Worthwoods, on the playground, in the classroom, even during the long walks to and from school with Todd and the other neighborhood kids. These friendships were the kind of bonds that form when children grow together, not just in years, but in spirit.

The faculty adored him, and it wasn't just lip service. They had told Judy time and time again that Jimmie was a model student: diligent, kind, eager to help, and never one to be defeated by a challenge. Socially, he thrived. He had an ease in conversation that drew people in, and a self-confidence that grew not out of arrogance but out of resilience.

When the principal called his name, "James Valentine," the applause thundered. Judy's hands clapped until they stung, and Dad's deep whistle cut through the noise. Jimmie rose, his cane clicking gently against the polished wood of the stage as he walked in a straight, deliberate line to accept his certificate. The pride in the room was palpable, and when he returned to his seat, Todd thumped him on the shoulder and whispered, "You nailed it, Jimmie."

But behind the scenes, there was someone else who deserved recognition, Leslie Williams, Jimmie's resource room teacher. Leslie wasn't just a teacher; she was an innovator, always searching for tools to help her students not only survive but thrive. She had introduced Jimmie to an athletic marvel: the "beep ball."

One afternoon in early autumn, she had gathered a group of students in the schoolyard, Jimmie among them, and produced what looked like an ordinary Clincher softball.

"This isn't just any ball," she explained, holding it up. "It has a beeper inside. You'll be able to hear it when it's moving."

Jimmie leaned forward, curiosity lighting his face.

"Go on, toss it," Leslie said.

Todd threw the ball lightly toward Jimmie. The faint beeping guided his ears. Jimmie reached out, and though he missed the first attempt, he adjusted quickly. The next time the ball came, he caught it clean in his hands.

"Yes!" Todd shouted.

Leslie clapped her hands. "See? Perfectly possible."

Before long, they were playing a full game. Jimmie, with his natural coordination and sheer determination, amazed everyone. When it was his turn to bat, he stood at the plate, listening intently to the rhythmic beeping as the ball approached. His swing was timed a split-second late, but on the third pitch he connected, the thud echoing across the field.

"Run, Jimmie!" the kids screamed.

And he ran. Straight as an arrow, no hesitation. Leslie would later comment, "Jimmie runs the straightest line of anyone I've ever seen out here."

That moment stuck with him. It wasn't just about a game; it was proof that the world could adapt, and that he could still be part of it fully.

***

The joy of graduation quickly gave way to the next big decision: high school. And here, Judy's tireless energy shone through. She poured over brochures, visited schools, and grilled administrators. But the options were slim.

The local high schools were overcrowded, underfunded, and most importantly, lacked any meaningful resources for the blind. Worse, they required long bus rides that would eat up hours of Jimmie's day. Judy refused to let her son's education fall into the cracks of a failing system.

"I won't settle," she told Dad one evening, her voice firm as they sat around the kitchen table. "He deserves more than a place to sit in a classroom. He deserves a school where he's seen, where he belongs."

Dad nodded, though his practicality sometimes clashed with Judy's vision. "We just need to be realistic, Jude. The closer the school, the better. I don't want him spending half his life on a bus."

But Judy had already unearthed a possibility. Catholic Charities in Chicago had a program that could provide all of Jimmie's textbooks in braille at no cost. The key was finding a school willing to partner with them.

She found one in the heart of the city: Holy Name Cathedral High School. The Sisters of Charity of the Blessed Virgin Mary, known affectionately as the BVMs, were renowned for their dedication to education. And when Judy explained Jimmie's situation, their response was immediate and enthusiastic.

"We would be honored to welcome James into our community," Sister Margaret had said, her tone both warm and decisive. "Every student has gifts. We will make sure his are not overlooked."

It was, as Judy put it later, "a match made in heaven."

***

But this decision also meant uprooting their lives once more. After ten years in Worth, it was time to move. The family chose something radically different: a brand-new high-rise condo on Lake Michigan, just east of the Loop.

The day they moved in, Jimmie pressed his hands against the cold glass windows that stretched floor to ceiling, marveling at the distant shimmer of the water.

"It sounds alive," he whispered as the muffled crash of waves echoed faintly from the shore.

"It *is* alive," Judy said, smiling as she unpacked boxes. "That lake's going to be part of our lives now."

The condo itself felt like a leap into the future. Gleaming marble floors, stainless steel fixtures, elevators that hummed like giant mechanical bees. Their old house with its brick walls and neighborhood yards had been traded for a vertical village in the sky.

For Jimmie, it was another challenge in mobility. Gone were the quiet, stone-covered streets of Worthwoods. Now, elevators, lobbies, and bustling downtown streets stretched before him.

"We'll take it one step at a time," Judy reassured him.

And as always, Catholic Charities stepped in, arranging for a specialized bus to pick Jimmie up each morning and bring him home after school.

***

The move brought big changes for everyone.

Judy, freed from her old work routine, threw herself into volunteerism with unbridled passion. The Art Institute of Chicago, Shedd Aquarium, Field Museum, Cultural Center, all became her playground. She delighted in the idea of being surrounded daily by history, art, and science, and she shared each detail with Jimmie in the evenings.

"Today," she told him once, "I helped a group of children stare up at Sue, the T. Rex skeleton at the Field. You could almost feel their jaws drop."

Jimmie grinned. "I want to hear about Sue, too."

Dad, on the other hand, loved the practicality of city living. His two-hour commute, an exhausting routine of highways, traffic jams, and late arrivals, vanished overnight. His office in the Loop was now a fifteen-minute walk. With a kind of glee he hadn't shown in years, he sold the family car.

"You wouldn't believe how much money we're saving," he announced. "Insurance, gas, repairs, parking. It's a whole new world."

"You just don't want to parallel park anymore," Judy teased.

But perhaps the biggest change was for Jimmie. Transitioning to Holy Name Cathedral wasn't just about academics, it was about carving out a place for himself in a new, bustling environment.

The first day, the air was thick with nerves. Judy fussed over his uniform, adjusting the tie until Jimmie finally groaned, "Mom, I can tie it myself."

"I know," she said softly, smoothing the fabric anyway. "I just… want it perfect."

The bus ride into the city was filled with the hum of voices, brakes squealing, horns blaring outside. Jimmie sat quietly, tapping his cane lightly against his shoes, rehearsing the layout of the school in his mind from what Judy had described.

When they arrived, Sister Margaret greeted him at the entrance. "Welcome, James," she said warmly. "We're so glad you're here."

The hallways echoed with footsteps, lockers clanging shut, laughter bouncing from every corner. It could have been overwhelming, but Jimmie's posture remained steady. He was here not as a visitor, not as a boy with limitations, but as a student, just like everyone else.

And so began a new chapter. Worthwoods had given Jimmie roots, but Holy Name would give him wings.

The family adjusted to life by the lake, Judy to her new roles in the cultural institutions, Dad to his newfound freedom, and Jimmie to the bustling energy of a city school.

But what tied it all together was the sense of adventure. They were no longer a family defined by limitations or obstacles. They were explorers in their own right, carving out new paths, adapting, growing.

And through it all, Jimmie's resilience, optimism, and quiet determination remained the compass guiding them forward.

Chapter 16

The move to Harbor Point felt like stepping into another world. Rising fifty-four stories above Lake Shore Drive, the tower overlooked the restless sweep of Lake Michigan and held within it a self-contained city: an indoor pool, racketball courts, a fitness center, a small grocery, a dry cleaner, even a sauna. For most residents, it was convenience. For Jimmie, it was freedom.

Blindness didn't shrink his world here; it expanded it. Every sound, scent, and echo became a landmark on the map he carried in his mind. The lobby announced itself with the soft whoosh of revolving doors, shoes clicking across marble, and the scent of polished brass. The elevators, six in all, were marked in braille, their hums and pauses familiar music to him. By the time the doors opened on the thirty-first floor, he already knew he was home, greeted by the muffled buzz of televisions and the faint aroma of dinners drifting through the corridor.

The staff treated him like family. Security guards called out greetings, maintenance men explained their tools as he ran his fingers over them, and grocery clerks placed peaches in his palm with a smile. Purchases went on the family account until his father reminded him, firmly, that freedom did not mean carte blanche.

Beneath the tower stretched ten floors of storage rooms and maintenance corridors, confusing to most but alive with echoes Jimmie understood. He roamed them like a cartographer, mapping every turn.

Still, the building was only part of it. What mattered most were his friends, Mario Contreras and Elegio "Hank" Crespo. Mischievous but loyal, they treated him not as fragile but as one of their own. Together, they laughed in the recreation rooms, planned adventures, and reminded Jimmie of a truth he carried quietly: Harbor Point wasn't just a building. For him, it was a fortress, a playground, and a stage where he belonged.

***

Jimmie's world would have been rich enough within the walls of Harbor Point, but what made it truly alive were the friends who came to share it with him. Mario Contreras and Elegio "Hank" Crespo were classmates at school, both from families who valued hard work and respect but carried themselves with a touch of streetwise ease. They weren't troublemakers, not really, but they knew more of the world than Jimmie did, and that difference pulled them together.

Mario was the joker. His laugh came easily, sharp and bright, like a crack of chalk on the blackboard. He was quick with comments, forever nudging situations into humor. He had a knack for spotting what adults missed, how the nun at the front of the classroom hummed under her breath, or the way one teacher's shoes squeaked louder when he was angry.

Hank was steadier, broad-shouldered and quiet until he had something worth saying. His friends called him "old man Hank" when he slipped into seriousness, but they respected him. He wasn't just worldly, he was observant. When Hank spoke, even Jimmie leaned in, sensing the weight behind his words.

The first time Mario and Hank visited Harbor Point, they couldn't stop gawking. The sheer size of the lobby made them whisper under their breath, and when the elevator doors opened with a soft chime, Mario elbowed Hank and muttered, "Man, this is like a hotel."

Jimmie smiled, running his fingers over the braille beside the button panel. "It's just home," he said.

"Home?" Mario snorted. "Jimmie, my whole building could fit into your lobby."

When they reached the thirty-first floor, Jimmie led them with confidence. His hand brushed the wall lightly, and his steps were firm, guided by memory. Hank watched closely, impressed by the ease with which Jimmie moved. "You know this place better than anyone," he said.

"Better than most sighted folks," Jimmie replied with quiet pride.

Soon, Harbor Point became their clubhouse. After school, the boys sprawled in the recreation areas, playing cards on tables that smelled faintly of polish, or listening to the rhythmic slap of swimmers below in the pool. Jimmie didn't play racketball, but he loved the sound of it, the sudden explosive *pop* of the ball against the wall, the scuff of sneakers chasing after it, the heavy breathing of players as the game wore on.

Sometimes, they descended into the lower ten stories, the hidden labyrinth of storage and service rooms. There, the building transformed into something secret, far from the polished lobbies. The air was cooler, tinged with the metallic scent of machinery and the mustiness of stored furniture. Their footsteps echoed differently in each passage.

Mario once dared, "Bet we can find a shortcut nobody knows about."

"You'd get lost in two minutes," Jimmie shot back, grinning. "I'll get us there faster."

Hank smirked. "What, you've got it all memorized?"

Jimmie tapped the wall with his knuckles, listening to the echo. "Every corner. Every sound. It's like a map in my head."

The boys followed him, skeptical at first, but Jimmie navigated turns with ease, counting steps, listening to faint machinery hums, identifying the change in acoustics when a hallway opened into a larger room. When they finally emerged into the loading dock, Mario whistled.

"Okay, you're the king down here," he admitted. "We'll follow you next time."

From then on, the labyrinth was their shared territory. They gave names to certain corners, "The Echo Room," "The Freezer Hall," "The Ghost Corridor" and laughed when others at school couldn't believe how much they knew about the inner bones of Harbor Point. More than once, security guards chuckled and asked, half-serious, for their advice about blind spots in surveillance or doors that didn't lock properly.

Back upstairs, Jimmie's apartment became the social hub. His parents encouraged it, relieved that their son had found boys who treated him as an equal. On weekends, classmates rode the CTA bus straight to Harbor Point's entrance. Some came wide-eyed, unused to such luxury. For kids living in cramped inner-city apartments, the indoor pool and racketball courts were marvels.

One Saturday, as Mario leaned back in a lounge chair near the pool, he looked around and said, "You realize everyone wants to be part of your crew, right?"

Jimmie shook his head, smiling faintly. "They just like the pool."

"No," Hank said firmly. "They like *you*. The pool's just the bonus."

The words sank deeper than Hank probably knew. For all the confidence Jimmie projected, he was never unaware of how others saw him, different, fragile, sometimes an obligation. With Mario and Hank, he wasn't a burden. He was one of them.

And soon enough, the three of them would test just how far that bond could go.

***

The idea began as a whisper, the sort of thought that slips between teenagers before anyone is brave enough to say it out loud.

Mario was the one who finally did. Sitting at the back of the classroom, he leaned close and murmured, "Cubs are playing this afternoon. Bleacher seats. What do you say we… you know… not go to algebra?"

Hank shot him a look, half amused, half cautious. "Cut class?"

Mario grinned. "Exactly. Come on, we've been perfect angels all semester."

Jimmie, who sat between them, tilted his head. "You're serious."

"As a home run in the ninth," Mario said. "What do you think?"

For a moment, Jimmie hesitated. Rules carried weight for him; they kept the world structured. But the thought of Wrigley Field stirred something inside him. The roar of a crowd, the organ music, the rhythm of a live game, he had heard about it all but never felt it himself.

"Alright," he said finally. "Let's go."

By the time the lunch bell rang, the plan was sealed. They slipped out with the crowd of students and made their way toward the "L." The clatter of trains filled the air as they reached the platform, the metallic screech of brakes and the electric hum of cars overhead. Jimmie tapped his cane lightly, following the vibrations through the concrete.

Mario clapped a hand on his shoulder. "This way, champ. Doors are open."

The train lurched forward, rattling along its tracks, and Jimmie gripped the pole, his body swaying with the rhythm. He could feel the energy of his friends beside him, Mario restless, humming a tune under his breath, Hank steady but smiling, eyes surely scanning the other passengers.

When they stepped off near Wrigley, the world changed. The air thickened with the smell of hot dogs, roasted peanuts, and spilled beer. Voices rose in waves, vendors shouting, fans laughing. Jimmie inhaled deeply, smiling.

"Smells like baseball," he said.

"Wait until you *hear* it," Hank replied.

Inside the stadium, the bleachers vibrated with noise. The organ pumped out a cheerful riff, followed by the collective swell of fans chanting. Every crack of the bat was a thunderclap. Jimmie sat between his friends, his hands gripping the edge of his seat, his whole body tuned to the game.

Mario leaned in, narrating with excitement. "That one's gone high… way high… center field! Man, he caught it right at the wall."

Jimmie laughed, the picture clear in his mind. "I can feel it in the crowd," he said. And it was true, the disappointment was like a ripple in the air, thousands of voices sighing at once.

In the seventh inning, something unexpected happened. A cameraman pointed his lens toward the bleachers, capturing the sea of fans. For a split second, Mario and Hank were on the big screen, their faces lit with grins. Jimmie, sitting between them, leaned forward, confused by their sudden hush.

"What is it?" he asked.

"You're not gonna believe this," Mario whispered, laughter barely contained. "We're on TV. Like… right now."

Hank groaned. "If the nuns see this, we're dead."

Jimmie chuckled. "Relax. What are the chances?"

But the unease lingered. As the game wound down and the Cubs pulled off a narrow win, the boys' excitement carried a shadow. They rode the "L" back with quieter voices, Mario's usual banter subdued.

The next morning confirmed their fears.

The principal's office smelled faintly of old books and furniture polish. The three of them stood in a row, shoulders straight but hearts thumping. Across the desk sat Sister Margaret, her hands folded, her eyes sharp.

"Imagine our surprise," she began, her voice measured, "when, during yesterday's game, several of the sisters recognized three of their students enjoying themselves in the bleachers."

Mario shifted uncomfortably. Hank stared at the floor. Jimmie felt the silence stretch, heavy and accusing.

Sister Margaret continued. "Your punishment will be service at the Cardinal's mansion in Lincoln Park. Maintenance, errands, whatever is required. Perhaps a day of labor will remind you of your responsibilities."

Mario exhaled, half relieved, half annoyed. "Could've been worse," he muttered when they left the office.

Hank raised an eyebrow. "She still might make us scrub the toilets."

Jimmie only smiled faintly, tapping his cane against the floor. "At least we got the game."

And in truth, he didn't regret it. The stadium still echoed in his memory, the chants, the organ, the electric tension of every pitch. For Jimmie, the punishment felt small compared to the gift of that afternoon.

***

The Cardinal's mansion in Lincoln Park stood like a relic of another time. High stone walls framed the grounds, and the front gates creaked open as if announcing their trespass. The building itself loomed heavy and silent, its brick walls weathered by decades of Chicago winters. For Mario and Hank, the place was intimidating. For Jimmie, it was something else entirely: a chorus of echoes, scents, and textures, each turn of the corridor telling him where he was.

The boys were handed over to a supervisor, a thin, bespectacled man with a clipboard and little patience for teenage antics. "You three," he said curtly, "will spend the day assisting with maintenance and cleaning. No fooling around. You work until I say you're done."

"Yes, sir," Hank muttered, his tone respectful.

Their first task was polishing the long marble floors of the entry hall. Buckets of soapy water and thick brushes were placed in front of them. Jimmie knelt, running his hand across the cool stone, feeling where dust had gathered. His brush rasped against the marble in steady strokes, water sloshing as he worked.

Mario groaned, his voice echoing dramatically off the high ceilings. "We cut class for baseball, and now we're scrubbing floors like monks. Fantastic."

"Better than detention," Hank replied, though his breathing was already labored.

Jimmie grinned, sweat beading on his forehead. "At least the floor tells you when you're done. Smooth under your brush? Move on. It's not so bad."

By midday, they were sent upstairs with rags and buckets to dust and polish the mansion's endless hallways. Jimmie tapped his cane along the baseboards, locating side tables and chairs. His fingers skimmed across carved wood, tracing intricate patterns before he wiped them clean. He worked by touch, careful and deliberate, while Mario and Hank raced ahead, their laughter echoing through the corridors.

In one room, sunlight streamed through stained glass, casting patterns on the floor. Jimmie couldn't see them, but he could feel the warmth shift across his face.

Mario leaned out the window. "Hey, you can see the whole park from here!"

Hank nudged him. "Shut it, before the guy with the clipboard hears."

Jimmie smiled faintly. "Describe it."

Mario turned, his voice softening. "Big old trees, leaves just turning gold. A few joggers. The lake glinting way off."

Hank added, "It's peaceful. Makes you forget we're working off a punishment."

Later, they were tasked with hauling boxes from the basement. The air there was thick with dust, the scent of old wood and forgotten paper. Jimmie carried lighter loads, guided by Hank's steady instructions. The stairs creaked under their weight, and Mario, always restless, pretended to stumble dramatically.

"Careful!" Hank barked. "You'll break your neck."

"Or the Cardinal's boxes," Jimmie added with a laugh.

By late afternoon, their arms ached, their backs were sore, and their clothes carried the mingled scents of polish, dust, and sweat. Yet, despite the labor, none of them felt crushed by the punishment. In fact, it stitched them closer together.

As they left the mansion, the supervisor finally nodded, though his voice remained stern. "Not bad for a group of boys who thought the rules didn't apply to them. Maybe you learned something."

Mario muttered under his breath as they stepped into the fading light. "Yeah… never sit in the bleachers where the TV cameras can find you."

Hank chuckled, shaking his head. "Lesson learned."

Jimmie tapped his cane lightly, the rhythmic sound echoing in the evening air. "Still worth it," he said quietly.

Neither Mario nor Hank disagreed.

***

Back at school, word spread quickly. The punishment at the Cardinal's mansion became part of the lore among their classmates. Most kids would have sulked or kept it quiet, but Mario and Hank told the story with enough dramatic flair that it sounded more like an adventure than discipline. The image of three boys, heads bent over marble floors in one of Chicago's grandest homes, struck everyone as both hilarious and oddly impressive.

For Jimmie, this shift was significant. Too often, kids his age treated him with caution, unsure how to relate to someone who couldn't see. But after the mansion episode, the trio was seen less as a curiosity and more as a group, tight-knit, mischievous, and full of stories worth retelling.

Part of their draw was Harbor Point itself. Jimmie's address carried weight: a fifty-four–story tower that gleamed against the lakefront skyline, filled with luxuries most kids only saw on TV. When classmates were invited to visit, they couldn't hide their awe. The lobby with its polished floors, the sound of water splashing in the indoor pool, even the steady whoosh of the elevators rising thirty-one stories, all of it left an impression.

Jimmie knew his advantage wasn't just the building's amenities. It was the way Harbor Point gave him freedom. In winter, when the city streets were slick and bitterly cold, he could still navigate a world within walls: the grocery store with its earthy scent of fresh produce, the dry cleaner's sharp tang of pressed fabric, the echoing courts where rubber balls cracked like gunfire. His cane tapped steadily, tracing routes through hallways he knew better than anyone. When visiting friends marveled at the place, he simply guided them, showing that his blindness didn't cage him; here, it gave him a kingdom of familiarity.

Mario and Hank reveled in the attention too. They weren't just Jimmie's friends anymore, they were his partners in exploration. Together, the three roamed not just the recreational floors, but the hidden labyrinth of storage and maintenance corridors. Security guards sometimes called them over, half-joking, half-serious, to ask how trespassers might sneak in unnoticed. The boys laughed, offering advice like seasoned consultants.

Other kids began angling for invitations. "When can we swim at your place?" someone would ask Jimmie in the cafeteria. "Do you really have a court inside the building?" another would press. The envy was open, but it didn't bother Jimmie. For once, he wasn't seen through the lens of his disability but through the aura of his friendships and his home.

His parents noticed too. Though cautious about spoiling him, they encouraged the visits, knowing how much it meant. They even teased him gently about the new rule Dad had put in place: no endless "charging" at the grocery store. "You can't treat it like your personal buffet," his father joked, though the twinkle in his voice softened the warning.

For Jimmie, the friendships were never about prestige or perks. What mattered most was that Mario and Hank never treated him as fragile. With them, he could share in laughter, in secrets, in the risk of getting caught at a Cubs game, or in the drudgery of polishing marble floors. They walked beside him not as protectors but as equals.

At night, as the city lights flickered through the blinds of the thirty-first-floor apartment, Jimmie often lay awake, cane resting by his bedside. The hum of traffic far below, the occasional thrum of the elevators, and the muffled laughter of his friends down the hall told him he wasn't alone. His world might be different, but it was full, textured, and alive.

And in that world, he wasn't just the blind kid. He was part of a trio, respected, envied, and, in their own way, legendary.

Chapter 17

Over the years, as Jimmie's swimming skills improved, the Harbor Point pool became more than just a place for exercise; it became a stage for discovery. The shimmering blue water was a second home, familiar and inviting, and Jimmie, with each stroke, grew more confident in his own strength. Swimming, once a challenge, had transformed into a source of freedom.

It was during this time that something unusual happened: Jimmie began to take an interest in SCUBA. His father, who had already been certified through the YMCA's SCUBA program, recognized the seriousness of this interest. Yet there was something extraordinary about it. For most swimmers, diving beneath the surface with heavy tanks and complex regulators was a challenge of skill and endurance. For Jimmie, however, there was an entirely new dimension to consider.

In water, gravity releases its grip. The body floats in neutral buoyancy, weightless and untethered. Without the anchor of sight, there is no horizon, no point of reference. Up and down blur into a single, endless direction. This was where danger lived, in the disorienting silence of the deep. And yet, this was precisely what fascinated Jimmie.

It wasn't just the equipment that caught his attention, though the tanks, regulators, fins, and masks certainly intrigued him. It was the science, the challenge, the puzzle of it all. The physics behind diving, the way pressure shaped the body and the air we breathe, was like a hidden code to be solved. Where others might have felt only caution, Jimmie felt curiosity. The unknown did not push him back; it pulled him closer.

Sensing this pull, his father reached out to the YMCA and asked if one of their instructors might be willing to hold a SCUBA certification class in the Harbor Point pool. To his relief, the answer came back yes. Lou Nessler, an instructor, agreed to take on the course. A notice went into the Harbor Point newsletter, complete with the price and scope of the training. The response was better than expected. Enough residents signed up to make the class possible. And at the heart of it, ready and eager, was Jimmie.

This was the beginning of something that would not only test his endurance and intellect but also reveal his determination to those around him. The pool, once a place of practice, was about to transform into a classroom of pressure, breath, and survival.

***

One of the first lessons Lou Nessler introduced in the Harbor Point pool was not about how to strap on a tank or how to clear a mask. It was about physics. SCUBA, at its core, is not just an adventure sport but a living demonstration of science in action. And Jimmie, who had always been drawn to understanding how things worked, absorbed every word.

The principle at the center of it all was Boyle's Law. It was the kind of concept often found in a high school physics textbook, but here, in the pool, it was more than theory; it was life and death. The law states that for a fixed amount of gas at constant temperature, the volume of that gas is inversely proportional to the pressure applied to it. In simple terms: the deeper you go, the greater the pressure, and the smaller the volume of air.

Jimmie listened intently as the example was given. At the surface, the pressure on the human body is one atmosphere. Descend thirty-three feet underwater, and that pressure doubles. A balloon filled with one cubic foot of air at the surface would shrink to half its size at that depth. Tanks filled with air at surface pressure would behave the same way when carried down into the water.

The danger lay not only in going down but in coming back up. If a diver inhaled air at depth, then rose to the surface while holding their breath, that same air would expand again, doubling in volume as the pressure was released. Inside the human body, this expansion could rupture lungs in an instant. The rule was absolute: never hold your breath on ascent. Always exhale. Always let the body and the air adjust together.

For most beginners, these rules were intimidating, but Jimmie was fascinated. The invisible forces of physics, the equations he could imagine and recite in his mind, gave structure to the unseen world beneath the surface. Diving was no longer simply about moving through water; it was about understanding the relationship between body, breath, and pressure. It was about respecting laws that could not be bent.

There was, however, an additional challenge unique to him. Without sight, the disorientation of buoyancy could be perilous. Which way was up? Which way was down? Sighted divers relied on visual cues, the shimmer of light above, the darker depths below. For Jimmie, those markers did not exist. To solve this, a simple but vital tool was added to his training: a weighted rope tied to his belt. The feel of the metal weight pulling downward gave him the answer that others could see, but he could only sense. It became his compass, silent and dependable, ensuring that even in the weightless confusion of water, he always knew where the surface waited.

While others treated diving as recreation, for Jimmie it was more than that. It was discipline. It was science. It was a challenge that asked him to master his body, his breath, and the elements themselves. And with every lesson, he showed that he was not only capable but determined to succeed.

***

Certification came slowly, step by step, but each step carried weight. Jimmie memorized the sequences for assembling and disassembling his gear. He practiced clearing water from his mask, practiced breathing calmly through a regulator, practiced sharing air with a buddy in simulated emergencies. Where others relied on quick glances and hand signals, Jimmie relied on memory, touch, and steady repetition.

When the day of his certification arrived, Lou Nessler and the examiners looked on with quiet admiration. They saw not just a student but someone rewriting the very expectations of the sport. Jimmie completed every requirement, every drill, and did so with determination that left the instructors impressed.

Recognition came quickly. At the 1980 Presidents Night, hosted by the Chicago Metropolitan YMCA SCUBA Diving Council, Jimmie was awarded their Distinguished Service Award. The inscription read: *"For his dedication, determination, and inspiration to all who dive."* Those words were not only engraved in bold lettering but also repeated in braille on the plaque, making it a rare award that spoke to him directly through touch.

The award was more than a token of achievement; it was a declaration that he belonged in the diving community. He was not just "the blind diver." He was Jimmie, a man with skill, courage, and respect for the water.

Soon after certification, he joined his father on dives beyond the pool, venturing into Lake Michigan. Beneath its cold, shifting surface, wrecks waited in silence, reminders of history preserved in rust and algae. For many, the lake was an unforgiving place to dive, its currents sharp, its temperatures frigid, but to Jimmie, the challenge was part of the allure. He descended with his weighted line, mapped the world with his hands, and learned to trust both the laws of physics and his own instincts.

What began as curiosity had now become a calling. He had earned not only a certification card but also the respect of divers across the city.

***

After Jimmie's certification, diving became more than a pastime, it became part of family life. His father began arranging trips that combined both sailing and SCUBA, the most memorable being in the Virgin Islands. They chartered sailboats, his dad listed as Captain, his mother recorded as passenger at customs, and Jimmie named as First Mate.

That title carried real responsibility. Each evening, after the day's sail and with the stars scattered across the Caribbean sky, the First Mate had his duty: to make certain the anchor was set properly. It wasn't enough for the chain to rattle out into the water; it had to bite into the ocean floor, secure against the restless push of tides and wind. For that, Jimmie relied on SCUBA.

With tank strapped firmly to his back and regulator steady between his teeth, he descended along the anchor line, fingers following the chain until he reached its resting place. Sand or coral told him whether the anchor had dug in or needed to be reset. Sometimes he would adjust it with his own hands, feeling the weight and drag of metal against the seabed. Only when he was sure the boat was safely moored did he return to the surface, signaling success.

For Jimmie, those nights were moments of independence. The Caribbean waters were warmer than Lake Michigan, and the dives were calmer, but they carried an equal measure of responsibility. In that quiet world below the waves, he was not sheltered or excused. He was relied upon. The safety of the boat and his family rested in his work as First Mate, and he carried the title with pride.

***

Back home in Chicago, sailing continued as a steady rhythm in Jimmie's life. The family held membership at the Columbia Yacht Club, located less than a block from Harbor Point. It was not a clubhouse in the traditional sense but a floating ship, moored permanently, its decks alive with conversation and the sound of rigging tapping against masts.

Membership gave them access to Monroe Street Harbor, where nearly four hundred boats swayed at moorings, their hulls creaking softly against the pull of Lake Michigan. For many, the harbor felt like a maze, docks repeating in near-identical rows, water shifting underfoot, voices echoing unpredictably across the slips. For Jimmie, it was a puzzle to be solved. Step by step, sound by sound, he mapped the yacht club and the harbor in his mind until he could move about with confidence.

Some of the other members' children noticed his independence and tried to unsettle him. They played tricks, testing the limits of what they assumed his blindness denied him. Yet Jimmie stood firm. He refused to be intimidated, meeting their challenges with steady resolve and quiet authority. In time, the teasing lost its sting, replaced instead by respect.

Within the Columbia Yacht Club, Jimmie was not seen only as a blind teenager but as a capable sailor, diver, and First Mate. He carried himself with assurance, not defined by what he could not see but by what he could do. The yacht club, with its clamor of activity and shifting sounds, became one more space in which he proved that blindness was no barrier to belonging.

***

Harbor Point had offered Jimmie more than a place to live, it had given him a foundation. The building, with its elevators marked in braille and its maze of storage corridors, had been his first training ground. There he learned orientation, persistence, and the quiet confidence that came from mastering his environment.

The swimming pool inside Harbor Point became the next stage, where hours of practice built skill, strength, and trust in his own body. SCUBA took it further, demanding not only discipline but an understanding of physics, safety, and responsibility. What began as curiosity grew into certification, recognition, and respect: from instructors, from the YMCA Diving Council, and from fellow divers who saw not limitation but ability.

Sailing in the Virgin Islands carried those lessons into open water. As First Mate, Jimmie bore responsibility that mattered each night when he descended to check the anchor. He shouldered it not as a symbolic role but as a duty essential to the family's safety. That reliance deepened his independence in ways no classroom could replicate.

At the Columbia Yacht Club and Monroe Harbor, he refined that independence in social ways, navigating docks, ignoring teasing, and standing firmly in who he was. In every space, from pool to harbor, he proved himself equal to the challenges, not by denying blindness but by meeting it with adaptability, knowledge, and determination.

By the time Jimmie received his Distinguished Service Award, engraved both in print and braille, the recognition felt natural. It was not a gift of sympathy but an acknowledgment of work, skill, and perseverance. Harbor Point had been the beginning, but water, whether in a pool, a lake, or the open sea, became the element through which Jimmie defined his strength.

Chapter 18

The four years at Holy Name Cathedral High School had not come easily for Jimmie. They were years measured not in semesters or report cards but in countless small struggles that piled one atop another. Every page of braille that passed beneath his fingertips represented not only knowledge gained but hours of labor, the patient reconstruction of sight into touch. Each bus ride, arranged through Catholic Charities, carried him across the city like a pilgrim moving from one world to another, the safety of home into the demanding order of the Sisters of Charity of the Blessed Virgin Mary. And every late night of study pressed against fatigue and silence, his room still awake long after others in the apartment building had surrendered to sleep.

Yet those years were not without gift. They offered him treasures he would never misplace: the discipline of the Sisters, who seemed to walk with one foot firmly on earth and the other planted in heaven. They demanded precision, memorized Latin, clean margins, punctual arrival, but balanced their authority with compassion, a hand resting lightly on a shoulder, a word of encouragement given at the right moment. His classmates, too, taught him lessons no textbook carried. They would not allow blindness to define him. They treated him not as fragile glass but as tempered steel, capable of both strength and resilience. And above it all, the rhythm of the Church nourished him. The liturgies, the incense drifting upward like whispered prayers, the quiet beauty of stained-glass windows he could not see but felt in the hush that surrounded them, these became sustenance as real as bread.

At home, his parents had always known their son was liked. Teachers would send notes remarking on his humor, his patience, his quiet determination that pulsed in him like a steady heartbeat. But it was not until the afternoon of his graduation that they understood the depth of admiration his peers held for him.

The auditorium that day was alive with expectation. It smelled of carnations pinned hastily to gowns, of waxed floorboards heated under the press of too many feet, of perfume dabbed behind ears by nervous girls smoothing their hair one last time. The air hummed with the restless shuffle of students waiting their turn. Parents leaned forward in their folding chairs, cameras ready, programs fluttering like paper wings. Teachers lined the sides of the stage, whispering instructions, their voices drowned by the low roar of anticipation.

Names were called one by one. Each announcement was met with polite applause, some bursts louder than others, a father's whistle or a mother's proud cheer punctuating the routine.

Then came his.

"James…"

The announcer had barely cleared the second syllable when the room erupted. The sound was sudden, volcanic, unstoppable. Cheers rolled down from the rafters as though the very beams of the auditorium had decided to shake loose. Applause thundered like rain hammering rooftops. Some students rose to their feet, shouting his name, clapping until palms stung red.

Jimmie, cane in hand, rose from his seat. For a heartbeat the world seemed to still, his parents exchanging startled glances, the pride swelling in their chests tangled with the sting of tears. They had expected recognition, of course, but something polite, perfunctory. This… this roar of affection, was something different. It was not courtesy; it was love. Not obligation; but respect. And carried within it was triumph, not only his but theirs, every sacrifice they had made transformed into a standing ovation.

He walked carefully across the stage, each step measured, the tap of his cane echoing against polished wood. The diploma, when it came into his hand, felt cool, almost fragile. He did not need to see the standing ovation; he felt it radiating toward him, a warmth more powerful than sunlight. For him, sound itself had always been map, guide, companion. On this day, sound became celebration.

***

Spring in Chicago had a way of reminding its citizens that life was precious. After months of gray sky and the punishing whip of wind off Lake Michigan, the city softened. Blossoms appeared along Michigan Avenue; children spilled from apartments into sun-soaked parks; street vendors returned, their carts clattering along sidewalks as though shaken awake from a long hibernation. Neighbors, once anonymous behind winter's closed doors, began greeting one another with nods, laughter, and cigarettes shared at stoop steps.

It was in this fragile season of renewal that Jimmie's family chose to celebrate his achievement. Chicago's summers were brief. June, July, August. Three months that demanded savoring, each day a gift not to be wasted.

"Where to?" his father asked across the dinner table one evening, the question tossed like an invitation.

Jimmie's answer came without hesitation. "The Greek place. The one with the patio. We should be outside."

And so they went, gathering not only parents and grandmother Dorothy but also Aunt and Uncle Lou and Wally, and close friends who had shepherded him through the trials of high school. At the long tables came plates of lamb rubbed with herbs, steaming moussaka layered thick, bowls of olives glistening with oil. Laughter rose and mingled with the scent of garlic and charred vegetables. The patio garden bloomed with vines curling upward into trellises, and beyond the brick walls the hum of the city carried on, a bus rumbling, a saxophone wailing faintly from some unseen corner.

But amid joy was absence. Jimmie's parents felt it keenly, as though their chairs had shadows. June and Bill gone, Mother Bennett too, and grandfather Jim Valentine. Their names floated silently at the edges of conversation, unspoken yet present. The living toasted, but the dead were never far from memory.

Still, there was wine. There was music. There was the satisfaction of marking victory hard-won through patience and endurance.

***

What came after? The question pressed harder now than ever before.

College had always been a possibility but never an ultimatum. His parents, both graduates of Knox College, spoke of Galesburg with fondness, weaving its campus into family lore. But in their late-night conversations, behind closed doors, they had agreed: "Let him decide."

Graduation came, and decision could no longer be deferred. His friends had already chosen their paths. Mario Contreras, restless and drawn to horizons beyond the city, set his sights on the Navy. Eligio "Hank" Crespo, steady and reliable, had a maintenance job waiting with the Chicago school district. Both paths were secure, honorable. Both made sense. College, by contrast, seemed distant, abstract, almost indulgent.

His parents nudged without pushing. One evening his father laid a brochure on the table, its glossy paper crackling as Jimmie's fingers explored its edges.

"What about Knox?"

"Small school," his mother added gently. "Fifteen hundred students or so. Professors who know your name. A place to learn how to learn, before you decide the rest."

Letters went back and forth. Knox's admissions office responded with confidence. Yes, they said, a blind student could be accommodated. Yes, logistics would be managed. Yes, he would be welcomed.

***

That summer they visited.

The campus in Galesburg lay under a wide sun, its heat softened by shade from century-old trees. Red-brick buildings stood dignified, their windows catching sky like mirrors. Jimmie walked the paths with his cane, counting steps, listening for echoes, mapping turns. He was writing, through sound and motion, his own private atlas of this new world.

They met faculty who had remained for summer session, professors who leaned forward in their chairs, their voices carrying not only curiosity but belief. Staff members spoke with assurance, their tone calm, steady, practiced.

The size of the college soothed him. Here were no vast lecture halls where a single student might vanish in a sea of hundreds. Here, learning was dialogue, a sharpening of thought against thought.

Dormitories clustered in small communities, four or five double rooms gathered around central living rooms, showers and toilets at one end. The design suggested fraternity, the slow weaving of friendship.

The dining hall lay only a block away, classrooms close, the gym within easy reach. Compact, manageable, yet broad enough to test his resolve.

Intimidation prickled at him. New streets, unfamiliar corridors, the maps he had built so carefully at Harbor Point would be useless here. But beneath that intimidation lay something stronger: resolve. He had navigated harsher terrain. He had survived more punishing tests. He was up to this.

That evening, sitting on the lawn with his parents as cicadas whined in the trees, he gave words to the decision already forming inside him. "It's a lot," he admitted, voice steady. "But I think I can do it."

His father's reply was simple, but carried weight. "Then let's apply."

∗∗∗

Weeks later the letter arrived, thick with promise. His mother slit it carefully and placed it in his hands. He traced the ridges of the paper while she read aloud.

"Congratulations. We are pleased to inform you…"

He didn't need the rest. The words were sunlight through blinds, a warmth spreading through chest and limbs.

He was going to Knox.

It was not only the next step in education. It was another leap in independence. Holy Name had shaped him, Harbor Point had anchored him, but Knox would be something different, an untested horizon. And like every challenge before, he was ready to face it. Step by step, cane tapping steady, he would walk into this new chapter.

Chapter 19

Jimmie's acceptance letter to Knox had arrived with the weight of possibility folded into a single envelope. To him, it meant a chance to step forward into the unknown, to test himself beyond the protective walls of home and Holy Name. To his parents, however, it was far more. Memories of their own college days at Knox rushed back, train rides through Illinois farmland, late nights of study, friendships forged for life. They were almost giddy, perhaps even more excited than Jimmie himself, and found themselves talking late into the evenings about the campus paths, the red-brick buildings, and the professors who had once challenged them.

The weeks leading up to the move blurred into a rush of preparation. Clothes were folded, labeled, and packed into suitcases. Special care was taken with Jimmie's sound equipment, his prized collection of tapes and players. He insisted that music would anchor him in the strange new world ahead, and his parents agreed. The small stereo, carefully wrapped in towels, went into the car first, almost like a ceremonial act, as if it were a guardian spirit leading the way to Knox. His cane, leaning against the doorway, seemed to carry a similar significance, both ordinary and extraordinary, a tool that would be his constant companion in this new chapter.

The car, a sturdy station wagon, was loaded until the springs groaned under the weight. Every crevice seemed filled with something essential: extra bedding, boxes of braille books, labeled folders of tapes, cans of soda for the road. Jimmie's mom checked and rechecked lists, while his dad adjusted the load with the precision of a ship captain balancing cargo. The morning they left, the family paused in the driveway, staring at the car packed to the roof. The sun was already bright, gilding the edges of the cornfields that framed the Chicago suburbs. It felt less like an ordinary drive and more like a pilgrimage.

The 200-mile trip from Chicago to Galesburg stretched before them. Unlike today's swift expressways, the route in those years meandered through towns, fields, and main streets. Route 34 was a living artery of the Midwest, and the family knew it well. They had traveled it many times for reunions, visits, and memories tied to Knox. Now, every familiar landmark carried a new weight, as though the road itself were ushering them toward a turning point.

They passed through Galva first, where the water tower rose above the town like a guardian, its chipped white paint reflecting the morning sun. Main Street seemed unchanged, brick storefronts, a diner with its screen door propped open, and the faint scent of frying bacon drifting on the breeze. Next came Altona, quiet and unassuming, its grain elevator standing sentinel against the flat horizon. The whistle of a distant freight train cut through the silence, reminding them of the iron pathways that once carried students, including Jim and Judy themselves, to Knox in earlier years.

Oneida was livelier, with children on bicycles darting across streets, waving as the family car rolled through. Each town blended into the next with familiar rhythm: a gas station with a rusted sign, a church steeple piercing the sky, fields of corn that rose higher than the windows of the car. The landscape was quilted with dairy farms and livestock pastures, dotted with the ubiquitous blue Harvestores silos that seemed to rise like monuments of Midwestern resilience. Jimmie, running his fingers across his cassettes, listened to his parents describe each sight. He grinned at their stories, filling in the images with his imagination. For him, the journey was painted not with visuals but with words, sounds, and the steady rhythm of the road beneath the tires.

Four hours later, they arrived in Galesburg, where the streets seemed quieter than the bustling city they had left behind. Knox's campus spread out in stately charm, red-brick buildings, towering oaks, and sidewalks that had carried generations of students into adulthood. For Jim and Judy, it was like stepping back into their own youth. They couldn't help but feel a strange mixture of nostalgia and anticipation as they turned into the driveway that would now be Jimmie's.

The dormitory awaited, a three-story building that stood both welcoming and intimidating. The proctor assigned to the floor greeted them with a clipboard in hand and a brisk smile. To their surprise, he explained that no roommate had been assigned to Jimmie. This meant free rein of the room, an unexpected gift that gave him space for his equipment, his books, and the quiet independence he would need. The building even had an elevator, a small detail that felt like a godsend to Jimmie's parents, who had worried about stairs and navigation.

Unpacking took hours. Each box opened seemed to release more than objects; it carried with it fragments of home. His stereo was set up in the corner, and the first tape clicked into place as though to christen the room. Clothes were folded into drawers, braille books lined up neatly, and his cane placed carefully by the bed. Jimmie's parents busied themselves with arranging, though their eyes often lingered on their son, watching his reactions. He was calm, but they knew beneath his steady demeanor lay a quiet storm of apprehension and excitement.

After the last box was tucked away, they set out to reorient Jimmie around campus. The walkways wound between red-brick halls shaded by centuries-old trees. They guided him to Seymour Hall, where food service bustled with the smell of coffee and fresh bread. They traced paths to the Science Building, the Library, Alumni Hall, and Old Main, the beating hearts of Knox. Each step was described in detail, each turn committed to memory. Yet even as they walked, Jim and Judy exchanged worried glances. They knew two hours of orientation could never substitute for the day-to-day challenges Jimmie would face. There was no Catholic Charities here, no nuns ensuring order and compassion. For the first time, Jimmie would stand on his own, supported not by institutions but by his own resilience and the goodwill of those around him.

The weight of this realization pressed on them. Failure was possible, failure had always been possible, but here, far from home, it loomed larger. Would he stumble? Would he withdraw? Would the college be enough to catch him if he faltered? They had placed their faith in him, and in the legacy of Knox itself, but faith did little to ease the knot in their stomachs. Jim thought back to the doctor he knew, a Knox graduate who had once insisted they should treat Jimmie naturally, as they would any child. That advice steadied him now, though doubt still crept in like an unwelcome shadow.

By evening, the family sat in Jimmie's room, the golden light of late summer slanting through the window. Conversation wandered between logistics and hopes. Jimmie tapped his cane on the floor thoughtfully, asking about the layout of Alumni Hall again. His parents answered patiently, but in their hearts they knew the real navigation ahead was not about buildings, it was about courage. When they finally stood to leave, Judy lingered at the doorway, memorizing the sight of her son in this new space. She felt the sting of tears but forced a smile. "You'll be fine," she said, more to herself than to him.

As the weeks unfolded, Jimmie began to carve his place socially. The start of the semester brought fraternity rush, and party invitations flowed freely. Curious students wanted to meet him, some out of genuine interest, others out of curiosity about his blindness. He handled both with quiet dignity, answering questions, laughing when laughter was appropriate, and brushing aside pity with firm humor. His father had ensured that Phi Delta Theta, his own fraternity, was aware of Jimmie. "I expect him to be a member," Jim had said firmly, leaving little room for doubt. The fraternity house, conveniently across the street from the dormitory, soon welcomed Jimmie as a pledge. Though the fraternity did not provide the logistical help Jim had hoped for, the gesture of inclusion mattered. It anchored Jimmie in the social fabric of Knox, giving him a foothold among his peers.

Still, the adjustment was not without strain. Nights alone in his room could feel cavernous, the silence pressing in when the stereo was off. Finding his way across campus sometimes ended in wrong turns or extra steps. Yet each misstep became a lesson, each day a new act of proving, to himself and to others, that blindness did not define his capacity. Knox was a liberal arts school, its very ethos built on the idea of learning how to learn. In that spirit, Jimmie was not just absorbing academic knowledge but mastering the deeper lesson of adaptation. He was, in every sense, learning how to navigate a world that was both welcoming and indifferent.

For his parents, each phone call home carried both relief and longing. They missed him fiercely, yet their pride swelled with every story he shared. In quiet moments, they admitted to each other that this new chapter was not just Jimmie's but theirs as well. They were learning, too, learning how to let go, how to trust, and how to believe in the strength they had always known their son possessed.

The chapter of Knox had only just begun, but already the pages were heavy with meaning. The journey down Route 34, the unpacking of boxes, the tentative steps across campus, all of it wove into the larger story of a young man stepping into his own. And though uncertainty still lingered, one truth was undeniable: Jimmie was ready to try, and trying was the bravest act of all.

<h1 style="text-align:center">Chapter 20</h1>

At Knox, Jimmie's arrival had carried the weight of expectation. His parents had trusted that the small size of the college, its promises of support, and its reputation for personal connection would make it manageable. But reality unfolded differently. The optimism of summer orientation, with its careful walks along shaded paths and promises from administrators, soon gave way to isolation.

The proctor's report confirmed what Judy and Jim feared most: Jimmie was staying in his room, not attending classes. The details arrived piece by piece, each one heavier than the last. He had no books to study. He did not know where the classrooms were. He lacked the mobility to cross the campus independently. Worst of all, he may not even have known which classes he was enrolled in.

It was the very nightmare his parents had whispered about in their kitchen late at night, afraid to speak too loudly, as though naming the fear would make it real. And now it was real.

The letter came before Thanksgiving. They unfolded the pages at the dining table, the words stark in their formality: Jimmie had not been attending classes. He was, in the quietest but clearest terms, failing. Judy pressed her hands against her face, fighting back tears, while Jim sat silent, the paper crumpling slightly in his grip. This was the confirmation of their worst fear, that their son had been sent into a world for which he had not been adequately prepared.

The failure was not his alone. Both parents felt it in their bones. Judy thought of her hours spent in volunteer work, the joy she had found in serving others, now soured by the thought that she had missed where she was most needed. Jim thought of his business, the pride he had taken in building it, and how easily he had let the busyness of life distract him. They had enjoyed their newfound freedom as empty nesters, dinners out, evenings quiet without responsibility, and now that freedom felt selfish.

They were not disappointed in Jimmie. They were disappointed in themselves. Somewhere inside, they admitted that part of their eagerness for Knox had been selfish too. They had dreamed of reliving their youth vicariously through their son, walking the same campus paths, hearing the same names of professors, feeling the continuity of legacy. And now those dreams crumbled alongside Jimmie's first semester.

The silence in the house that night was thick. They ate little. They said less. The disappointment was not sharp or angry; it was heavy, like a fog that settled in and would not lift. Jimmie was floundering, and they had to decide what to do next.

***

When Thanksgiving drew near, Jimmie's parents decided it was time for him to come home. The college had already made clear what they dreaded: his first semester was collapsing. There was no point in letting him linger in isolation until the holidays.

Jimmie himself suggested the Greyhound bus. The terminal on Randolph Street sat in the heart of the Loop, and it was practical, cheap, direct, manageable. For him, the idea carried a thread of independence: he could still travel like any other student returning home. For his father, the suggestion carried sorrow. The bus terminal was not the kind of triumphant homecoming he had once pictured for his son.

They lived on the far east end of Randolph, and when the day arrived, Jim walked on foot to meet him. The sidewalks of the Loop were alive with holiday bustle. Storefronts displayed early Christmas decorations, artificial snow, strings of lights, mannequins wrapped in scarves. Shoppers carried paper bags, their footsteps brisk in the November chill. Amid that energy, father and son finally met.

The sight was difficult for Jim. Jimmie emerged from the bus not with pride or confidence but with defeat in his shoulders. His cane tapped the pavement softly, each step measured, his suitcase hanging awkwardly from one hand. He had not made it, and the weight of that failure seemed to cling to him like the cold.

Jim greeted him with warmth, but behind the words was sadness. This was not anger, it was grief. He wanted to protect his son, but there was no shielding him from the truth. Both knew what had happened at Knox, and both felt the ache of disappointment.

Still, Jimmie clung to one note of pride: he had been accepted by his father's fraternity. That mattered. It was a sign that he belonged somewhere on campus, at least in spirit if not in classrooms. Perhaps he did not realize it, but his father was more proud of that acceptance than he was himself. For Jim, it symbolized continuity, a bridge between his own youth and Jimmie's attempt at independence. Even if academics had crumbled, that link stood firm.

The holiday passed quietly. Thanksgiving dinner came and went, rich with the familiar comfort of family rituals, yet shadowed by unspoken thoughts. Afterward, plans were made. The weekend after the holiday, they drove back to Galesburg.

The trip to Knox was heavy. The car seemed quieter than usual, the fields outside dull with the late-autumn gray. When they arrived, the task was simple but heartbreaking: pack up what remained of his semester. Clothes folded, belongings gathered, personal items restored to boxes and bags. Dorm walls that had once promised community now looked bare, indifferent.

Together, they brought him back home. His room, waiting as he had left it, became once again his anchor. The college chapter had ended before it began, and all of them felt the question rising: what now?

***

Back home, the air felt different. The silence of Jimmie's bedroom, familiar walls, shelves lined with tapes, the steady hum of the record player, was both comforting and accusing. Knox was over. The question pressed against every mealtime conversation, every quiet moment: what next?

Two avenues presented themselves, neither resembling the neat vision his parents once carried of a traditional college education.

The first was radio school. Jimmie had heard about a program in the downtown area, a small training center that specialized in broadcasting. For a young man who loved conversation, who had always been known for his wit, his voice, and his ability to engage people, it seemed practical. Radio required no sight, only sound, the very sense he had sharpened to an art.

But the challenge was not inside the school. It was in getting there. Mobility again became the obstacle. The building sat in the city center, about a mile or two from home. It wasn't a distance long enough for a bus ride, but far enough to be intimidating for someone navigating by cane. Once again, his father stepped in, guiding him along the route those first few times. The sidewalks of Chicago were never still, vendors calling out, horns blaring, strangers weaving past in unpredictable patterns. Jimmie learned the path one block at a time, listening to the rhythm of the crosswalks, memorizing the echo of certain corners, steadying himself against the thrum of the city.

After those early lessons, the responsibility became his. Each morning, he shouldered it himself, cane tapping, steps counted, ears alert. It was slow, sometimes frustrating, but every walk was a small act of independence.

The second path was music. Jimmie's drumming had grown sharper in recent years, his timing crisp, his sense of rhythm unshakable. A few friends in the neighborhood had a band, and he was welcomed into it. For him, it was more than just a pastime; it was an expression. For his father, it meant hauling drums in and out of the car, acting as the roadie on one-night gigs across the city. The venues were rarely glamorous: smoky bars, rented halls, basements humming with amplifiers. But they pulsed with energy, and Jimmie belonged there.

He never pretended the band would become a career. The gigs were temporary, fragile, one night at a time. But they gave him art. They gave him camaraderie. They gave him purpose in evenings otherwise clouded by questions about the future.

Through it all, his parents continued to wrestle with disappointment, not in him, but in themselves. They had pictured something else for their son, something closer to the paths they had walked. Yet what surprised them most was Jimmie's contentment. He was not crushed by Knox's failure. He was fun to be around, still eager to talk, always interested in music, radio, and the company of friends.

High school companions still called on him, folding him easily into their social circles. Family weekends remained lively. Though the trajectory had shifted, life still contained warmth, laughter, and possibility.

In the quiet moments, his father reminded him gently: "It's best to be independent, Jimmie. To be self-supporting, if you can. Build something for yourself." Jimmie nodded, already aware. He knew his future would never look like anyone else's. But he also knew he could carve a place for himself with his voice, his music, his presence.

And so, between the radio school mornings and the drum-laden nights, Jimmie began to stitch together a life beyond Knox, one measured not by what had been lost, but by what could still be built.

Chapter 21

It was 1984, and Chicago stretched out in its restless rhythm of steel and glass, of lake winds and looping expressways. For Jim, the city had been both anchor and cage. At forty-six, he had already given twenty-three years to the same company, climbing steadily but quietly, the kind of man who showed up early, stayed late, and kept the wheels turning even when others faltered. Yet years of loyalty had ended with disappointment. A major promotion had passed him by, and the silence that followed confirmed what he already suspected, he had reached the ceiling. His career in the Chicago office was stalled, if not finished.

Then the offer came. Another company, based in New York, wanted him. Not as a cog, not as a placeholder, but as Vice President of Sales. The title itself carried weight, promise, and recognition. Someone had noticed. Someone believed he was capable of more. It was a spark, and Jim knew sparks had to be tended before they died.

The decision, however, wasn't his alone. That evening in the Harbor Point condo, the family gathered. The building itself had become a world within a world, a high-rise that overlooked Grant Park and Monroe Street Harbor, where the lights of boats twinkled against the dark water and the hum of the city pressed faintly against the windows.

Judy sat upright, her eyes bright. To her, New York was not just a career move; it was an adventure. "You can't hesitate," she said firmly, her voice cutting through the low rumble of the city outside. "We should all go. Right away. Why wait?"

Jim, cautious by nature, leaned back, fingers steepled. His instinct was to go ahead first, to take the job, settle into the city, and then bring Judy and Jimmie once he understood the lay of the land. "Better to see how things are first," he said. "No sense in rushing."

But Judy would not hear it. To her, waiting meant missing out, and she had no intention of watching life unfold from the sidelines. "I won't sit here while you start a new life in New York. We go together."

The unspoken tension settled on Jimmie. At an age where independence and friendship meant everything, he was rooted to Chicago. The condo was more than walls, it was safety, it was familiarity. Every hallway, every echo, every turn of the stairwell was a map he had mastered. His friends were here too, the people who understood him, who had walked beside him through school and beyond. The idea of leaving all of it for New York, a city vast, chaotic, and unfamiliar, was not appealing.

The problem sharpened: how could they move forward without abandoning Jimmie?

The answer came with Dorothy. She had always been drawn to the energy of Harbor Point, the building's rhythm of community. When the proposal was made, that she move into the condo with Jimmie, each looking out for the other, she accepted without hesitation.

For Dorothy, the idea was not sacrifice but opportunity. Harbor Point offered her a rich life: weekly happy hours in the party room off the lobby, where neighbors mingled over cocktails and stories; a full-service grocery store built into the tower, its shelves always stocked; and the convenience of a bus stop right at the front door, granting her effortless access to the Loop. From her favorite chair by the window, she would have a front-row view of the city's life below, Grant Park stretching like a green quilt, Monroe Street Harbor sparkling with sailboats in the summer and resting silent in winter. "It's perfect," she said. "We'll take care of each other."

The plan eased the tension, though not completely. For Jim, there remained guilt. He knew Jimmie preferred Chicago, but he also knew opportunity like this rarely knocked twice. For Judy, there was only excitement. She imagined Broadway lights, galleries, the endless pulse of a city that never slept. For Jimmie, there was quiet acceptance. His independence was intact, and the presence of his grandmother promised companionship.

When the time came, Jim and Judy packed lightly. Only clothes, no furniture, no heavy commitments. Their choice was deliberate: this was reconnaissance, a first step. Yet even as they zipped the last suitcase, the air was charged with anticipation.

At O'Hare, as the plane taxied, Judy pressed her hand against Jim's. "This is it," she whispered. "The next chapter."

New York greeted them with noise. The airport was a storm of announcements, rolling suitcases, and cab drivers shouting over one another. The company had expected them to live on Long Island, closer to the factory and office. Suburbs, predictability, proximity, it made sense on paper.

But Judy's heart was never in the suburbs. She wanted the city itself, the heartbeat of Manhattan, the restaurants tucked into narrow streets, the theaters that lit up at night, the constant motion that marked every hour of every day. Jim, though cautious, found himself drawn in as well. They ignored the company's suggestion of Long Island and planted themselves firmly in the city.

For Jim, it was a professional rebirth. For Judy, it was adventure. For Jimmie, back in Chicago, it was stability on his own terms, with his grandmother by his side.

The crossroads of 1984 had set them on divergent but connected paths: Chicago's harbor for one, Manhattan's skyline for the other. Each carried its own challenges, its own promises. And though the family was split by geography, they were bound by choice, each step taken with the hope of building not just careers or routines, but a life worth living.

Chapter 22

It was 1987, a year that seemed to hum with the soft static of possibility. After several years in New York City, with a short business stint in Atlanta, Union Special had once again called Jim home, this time to Chicago, where an administrative management position awaited him. It was not just a return to a job but to a life that felt familiar and right. There was a quiet sense of restoration in the move, as though a long-unwritten chapter was finally resuming its lines.

When we arrived back at **Harbor Point**, the tall, curving residential tower that stood like a sentinel along Chicago's lakefront, it felt as if the building itself exhaled a welcome. Its glass facade reflected the restless waters of Lake Michigan, capturing the changing moods of the sky, slate gray at dawn, silver-blue by noon, and gold-flecked in the late afternoon. To live there was to exist between earth and water, always close to motion, to reflection, and to the wind that whispered through the Outer Drive.

Jim and Judy had missed this rhythm of life, the sound of the lake brushing against the breakwater below, the muted hum of the city beyond, the shimmering view of Navy Pier, which is north of Harbor Point. Chicago had a way of grounding us, even in its coldness. After years of being away, this was not merely a relocation; it was a homecoming.

Jimmie and Dorothy were delighted to be back as well. They preferred the comfort and familiarity of living with them in the condo, but as life settled into its patterns, they decided it was best to give everyone a bit more breathing room. They rented a small studio apartment within the same building so that Jimmie and Dorothy could maintain their independence while still being close enough for morning coffee or late-night chats. It was a practical solution but also one that respected the flow of the family life, connected, yet gently autonomous.

Chicago in the late '80s was an intriguing mix of industrial might and quiet reinvention. The skyline was a blend of sleek glass towers and sturdy brick buildings that told stories of an older, working-class city. From the high windows of Harbor Point, the view stretched out endlessly, a patchwork of streets, bridges, and moving headlights that pulsed like veins in the city's body.

Each morning began with the steady ritual of Jim's swim. The indoor pool at Harbor Point was enormous, encased in a glass atrium that allowed in the pale light of dawn. The smell of chlorine mingled with the crisp scent of lake air that sneaked in whenever the maintenance doors opened. Jim would swim lap after lap in clean, precise strokes, always steady, always deliberate. The water seemed to hold him in a state of calm focus, a meditative contrast to the structured world of corporate management awaiting him upstairs.

Jimmie, on the other hand, was not a morning person. His rhythm belonged to a different clock, one that came alive after noon and found its pulse in music. He had learned to swim years earlier at the Lincolnshire Country Club, and though he rarely joined his father for morning laps, he carried that same quiet competence in the water.

Jim had long noticed his son's natural sense of sound, the way Jimmie could identify the faint hiss of static between radio frequencies or tap out a rhythm with uncanny precision. It was Jim's idea that Jimmie should start thinking more seriously about a career in radio broadcasting. It wasn't just a job suggestion; it was a nudge toward a dream that had been waiting just beneath the surface.

Together, they began reviewing schools, programs, and possibilities. The greatest challenge wasn't interest; it was logistics. Getting Jimmie safely and conveniently to school had to come first. We still remembered the difficulties he faced earlier at Knox, where navigating from one place to another became an exhausting ordeal. This time, they wanted things to be simpler, smoother, more accessible.

They found a school less than a mile from Harbor Point, a manageable distance that gave Jimmie both independence and security. The route was simple enough: out the front door, along the Outer Drive, and a right turn toward the S-curve. The pathway hugged the lake, a long strip of pavement bordered by a guardrail on one side and the restless blue expanse on the other. It was safe, though often exposed to the whims of Chicago's weather, biting wind in winter, misty fog in spring, and the humid press of summer heat.

From the S-curve, a staircase descended to Grand Avenue. At the bottom, turning left led straight to the school's entrance. For several weeks, they walked that path together, sometimes in the early morning light, sometimes under the muted orange of streetlamps. Each walk was a quiet rehearsal, footsteps and conversation blending with the steady hum of the traffic above. By the time Jimmie announced that he knew the route well enough on his own, Jim realized those walks had become more than orientation; they were a bridge between past uncertainty and newfound confidence.

Outside school, Jimmie had another passion. Drumming. The rhythmic thump of his drum set became a familiar pulse in their home. He played in a small band that performed a couple of times a month, usually in local clubs or community gatherings. Jim proudly became his unofficial "roadie," hauling drums and cymbals into the van, helping with setup, and waiting near the bar while the band performed.

Those evenings had their own kind of beauty: dim rooms filled with neon light, the smell of beer and wood polish, and the syncopated sound of Jimmie's sticks against the drums. Jim would sit with quiet pride, watching his son in his element. Between sets, he might nurse a beer, chat with locals, or just listen, letting the music fold into the night.

The idea of expanding this passion into something bigger came naturally. Jimmie's audio and broadcasting studies began blending with his music, and soon, conversations in their condo turned toward the idea of opening a recording studio.

They began researching. The possibilities in Chicago were many; some studios were fully equipped and available for sale, complete with soundproofing, acoustics, and instruments. The temptation was strong, but so were the realities. The financial commitment was significant, and the operational costs, equipment maintenance, rent, utilities, and staffing added up quickly. Jim suggested they pause. The dream would stay alive, but the timing wasn't yet right.

While the studio plans were on hold, another kind of adventure found its way into their lives, one that would take Jimmie far deeper than sound waves ever could.

The Harbor Point pool, already central to their daily life, became the setting for an unexpected chapter. They learned about a YMCA-certified SCUBA instructor, Lou Nesslar, who offered diving classes right in the building's pool. The thought of learning to dive, of exploring the silent, suspended world beneath water, intrigued them all, but especially Jimmie.

They recruited a few other Harbor Point residents to join the class. The pool echoed with laughter and splashes as they all tried on their fins and masks for the first time. Lou was a patient, charismatic instructor, the kind of man whose calm demeanor immediately built trust. He had the quiet authority of someone who'd spent years underwater, his voice slow, deliberate, always carrying a note of reassurance.

From the very first session, Lou was taken with Jimmie. He noticed the fearlessness in him, the way he moved through the water without hesitation, as though he had known it forever. For Jimmie, the world beneath the surface was not unlike the world he already knew: *dark, murky, without sight*. But that darkness did not frighten him. It was familiar.

To help Jimmie orient himself underwater, Lou attached a weight about three feet long to his belt. It was *not* a safety anchor, it didn't rest on the pool floor. Instead, it served as a simple guide, giving Jimmie a tactile sense of *up* and *down* but offering no indication of *right* or *left*. Every dive was done in zero visibility, so Jimmie relied completely on his internal awareness, balance, and control.

There was no need to introduce night diving, because in truth, everything Jimmie did *was* night diving. Lou often said that while others trained to master darkness, Jimmie had already made peace with it. Underwater, he was calm, deliberate, and graceful. The other students learned to trust their eyes; Jimmie had learned to trust *everything else.*

There was never a gentle tug of a rope to lead him, no reassuring line to follow, only the rhythm of his breathing, the feel of the water pressing evenly against his body, and the faint sound of his own bubbles rising toward the surface.

When Lou later spoke of Jimmie's diving, he described it not as an adaptation, but as a revelation. "Most of us," he said, "lose our sense of direction when the lights go out. Jimmie never had that problem, because he never needed the lights to begin with."

Months later, word came from the Chicago Metropolitan YMCA SCUBA Diving Council that they wanted to honor Jimmie. On the evening of the President's Night, they attended the ceremony, a formal yet heartfelt gathering filled with divers, instructors, and families. The room buzzed with quiet admiration as Lou took the stage to speak about his students, saving Jimmie's story for last.

When he began describing Jimmie's journey, his skill, his fearlessness, and the way he inspired others, a hush fell over the room. Lou's voice softened as he said, "What Jimmie accomplished in that pool wasn't just a demonstration of technique. It was a demonstration of courage, of how limits exist only where we allow them to."

Then came the presentation: the Distinguished Service Award, inscribed with the words *"For his dedication, determination, and inspiration to all who dive."*

The applause that followed seemed to vibrate through the room. Jimmie stood proud, humble, radiant in the soft glow of the stage lights. Later, as the award was passed around the table, they turned it over and found that the back had been engraved in Braille, a gesture so thoughtful it left everyone speechless.

Life at Harbor Point settled into its own quiet rhythm. The building was more than a residence; it was a vertical community. The lobby always smelled faintly of fresh polish and coffee from the small café tucked near the entrance. Elevators chimed softly, carrying residents to their separate worlds.

From the condo windows, mornings began with the silvery shimmer of the lake stretching endlessly eastward. On foggy days, the horizon disappeared completely, and the city felt like an island floating in mist. At night, the lights of Navy Pier twinkled in the distance like a constellation anchored to the shore.

Winter was harsh but beautiful, the wind off the lake cut through even the thickest coats, and snow piled against the curved façade of the building. Inside, the pool steamed gently, a small tropical refuge from the world outside.

On weekends, we sometimes gathered with friends from the building, fellow residents who'd taken the SCUBA course or shared in Jimmie's adventures. The conversations drifted easily between work, music, travel, and the quirks of city life.

When people think of 1987, they might recall the music on the radio, the shoulder-padded fashion, or the early stirrings of a changing decade. For them, it was the year of returning home, to the city, to each other, to the steady pulse of life that had momentarily been scattered across states.

In the end, what stands out most is the way ordinary days carried quiet beauty. The sound of Jim's morning swim, the rhythmic drumming from Jimmie's room, the smell of chlorine mingling with lake air, the slow hum of the Outer Drive, all of it stitched together into the soft, enduring fabric of their family's story.

Chapter 23

By the time the chill of another Chicago winter crept in, Dorothy was finding it increasingly difficult to live on her own. The familiar walls that had once held laughter and warmth now echoed with the quiet ache of independence slowly slipping away. Even with Jimmie's gentle presence nearby, and Jim and Judy close within the same building, the day-to-day challenges were growing heavier. Small tasks that had once been routine, brewing her morning coffee, watering her plants, or walking down the hallway, had begun to feel like quiet battles.

Jim could sense that change was necessary. He approached it not with haste, but with care, poring over documents, touring retirement communities, studying financial details under the soft glow of the kitchen light that stretched into long evenings. He wanted the next step for his mother to feel like a continuation, not an ending. After weeks of quiet research and many conversations, he found a place that felt right: safe, dignified, filled with sunlight and soft laughter. Dorothy, with her characteristic grace, agreed.

When the day came, she moved to her new home without bitterness, her small collection of treasured belongings packed with careful hands. It was a transition marked not by loss, but by acceptance, a passage from one chapter of life to another. The family helped her settle in, arranging her favorite chair near the window and setting out framed photographs that captured decades of memories. The walls, bare at first, began to breathe again.

Her move brought another quiet transformation: Jim and Judy left their cramped studio apartment and returned to the two-bedroom condo. The building, with its familiar hum of the city and its view of Lake Michigan, once again became a family home.

Now, reunited under the same roof, Jim and Judy found a rhythm of living that blended their individual pursuits with shared joys. The condo seemed to come alive again, filled with the mingling sounds of music, laughter, and the faint rustle of lake winds that seeped through the windows.

Jimmie's circle of friends, Mario and Eligio in particular, became regular visitors. Their voices echoed in the hallways, bringing warmth and movement to the quiet moments. Mario's booming laughter and Eligio's gentle teasing became familiar sounds, so frequent that they began to feel like family themselves. The small gatherings often spilled into evenings filled with conversation and food, the scent of homemade meals blending with the lake air and city lights glowing beyond the glass.

For Judy, this chapter bloomed into one of deep artistic immersion. As a volunteer at the Art Institute of Chicago, she found herself surrounded by beauty and intellect. The museum's marbled halls, its soft lighting glinting off gilded frames, became a kind of sanctuary. She walked among the masterpieces of Monet, Renoir, and Degas, each brushstroke whispering the romance and melancholy of late 19th-century France.

Judy made close friends among curators and fellow volunteers, sharing conversations that intertwined between art and life. She also developed a keen connection with the staff of the Fashion Institute at the School of the Art Institute of Chicago, her eyes alight with fascination at the interplay of texture, form, and color. To her, fashion was not mere attire, it was moving art, sculpted by time, culture, and emotion. The hours she spent there filled her days with purpose and community.

Jim's world, meanwhile, was anchored not by marble halls but by the open expanse of Lake Michigan. He had long been a member of the Columbia Yacht Club, where the lake's restless waves were as familiar to him as the streets of the city. The sound of halyards tapping against masts, the smell of varnished wood and fresh water, the sight of sails straining in the wind, all stirred something deep within him.

Jimmie, too, had inherited this love of the water. Together, father and son spent long afternoons sailing the dinghies that danced across the harbor. But now, with Jim joining the Chicago Yacht Club, their adventures deepened. He bought a larger thirty-foot sloop, sleek and white, its polished deck glinting in the summer sun. They moored it at Monroe Street Harbor, right where the skyline met the horizon. From the windows of their condo, they could spot it, silent and steady, bobbing gently in the water like a promise.

Jimmie took naturally to sailing. His small hands gripped the ropes with growing confidence, and his eyes sparkled with concentration as he learned to trim the sails and adjust the heading to harness the shifting winds. For Jim, it was both pride and peace, to watch his son learn not only the mechanics of sailing but also the art of reading the lake, feeling its moods.

Summer days were long and golden. They filled them with the rhythm of the season: sailing whenever the sun smiled, and, as Judy often observed, "leaving just enough time to visit the Lincoln Park Zoo and smell the monkeys." It became a family joke, one that softened the edges of their structured days.

Yet, even in the joy of those months, there lingered the inevitable truth of Chicago's fleeting sailing season. By late August, the air grew cooler, the lake darker, and the sails had to be furled away. The family, unwilling to let go of the spirit of wind and water, found a new way to keep it alive.

They established what would become their annual winter pilgrimage to the Virgin Islands. It began as an idea, a way to escape the biting cold of Chicago and continue their shared love for the sea. Soon, it became a tradition.

Each year, as the city sank into snow, they would pack their bags and fly toward warmth and turquoise waters. In the Virgin Islands, time slowed. The days unfolded with the sun rising in gold and setting in deep coral pinks. They rented a sailboat and spent two blissful weeks island-hopping, drifting from one lush shore to another.

For Jim, it was a navigation dream, an easy kind of "eye-ball" navigation, where the islands were visible from the deck, and charts were more reassurance than necessity. He relished the simplicity of it: steering by instinct, reading the sea, guiding the vessel with quiet confidence.

For Judy, the magic lay on land. Each new island offered a fresh restaurant, each night a different flavor. She delighted in local dishes served under open skies, in laughter shared with strangers who quickly became friends, and in the feeling of air that never once bit with cold.

And for Jimmie, it was pure wonder. Every anchorage was a new challenge, every dive an adventure. He made it his ritual to plunge into the crystalline water each morning, diving deep to check the anchor's hold. Often, he would resurface with treasures, shells, bits of coral, and smooth stones, all tucked into his "goodie bag" like offerings from the sea itself. His eyes would gleam as he showed them to Jim and Judy, proof of his underwater explorations.

The boat, under starlit skies, became their floating home. The gentle rocking of the hull, the creak of the ropes, the salt drying on their skin, each sensation knitted them closer together. On calm nights, they would sit on deck, the ocean stretching endlessly around them, and talk about life in the soft glow of lantern light.

Back in Chicago, the rhythm of city life resumed, but something had changed. Their connection to the water, to one another, and to the world beyond the city's edge had deepened. The lake outside their window now felt less like a boundary and more like an invitation.

Dorothy, in her retirement home, remained a steady presence. Jim and Judy visited often, bringing stories and laughter from their adventures. She listened with pride, her eyes bright as she heard about the sailboat in the harbor, the friends who had become family, the art exhibitions and voyages that defined her children's lives.

There was something profoundly circular about it all. The family, once bound within the tight quarters of a studio apartment, now existed in a wider, freer rhythm, connected by water, by art, by memory, and by love.

Chicago, with its contrasts of wind and steel, art and water, had given them all a setting rich in both challenge and grace. In its summers, they found adventure. In its winters, they found escape. And through it all, they discovered that home was not merely a place, but a collection of moments, of shared laughter, quiet understanding, and the simple act of setting sail together toward whatever horizon awaited next.

Chapter 24

When the company asked Jim to take a new position at the factory in Huntley, northwest of Chicago, it felt like a turning of the page, one of those quiet shifts life makes without asking first. Huntley wasn't the Chicago skyline they were used to seeing out their windows. It was a place where open fields met concrete, where the air smelled faintly of rain and machinery, and where the sky seemed to stretch farther than it did in the city.

Jim accepted the role without hesitation, as he always did, steady, pragmatic, never afraid of responsibility. Still, there was a subtle awareness that this move would rearrange more than just his commute. It would reshape the rhythm of their days, the unseen threads that tied their family's life together.

Around this time, a different kind of change was stirring in workplaces across the country. The push for equal opportunity employment, especially for those with disabilities, was gaining real momentum. It wasn't just talk anymore; policies were shifting, attitudes softening, doors slowly opening.

Jim, seeing the world take these first steps toward inclusion, thought of Jimmie. His son had talent, curiosity, and a quiet determination that could outlast almost any obstacle. So one afternoon, with the kind of hope that fathers carry quietly in their chest, Jim walked into Human Resources and asked a simple question:

"Would there be a position here for my son?"

To his relief, the answer came back positive. Yes…there was space, and not just as a gesture of goodwill. They offered Jimmie a position as clerk and receptionist, with the full intention of helping him succeed.

For the company, it was a step toward inclusion. For Jim, it was something deeper, a bridge between opportunity and belief.

They worked together to set Jimmie up for success. Technology was evolving quickly in the late eighties, and it was remarkable what could be done with the right tools. The company installed a refreshable Braille display, a slim device that transformed digital text into a tactile landscape of raised dots. The Braille cells clicked faintly, like a heartbeat of information beneath Jimmie's fingertips.

There was also a screen reader, a steady, synthetic voice that translated the written word into sound. Instead of a mouse, Jimmie navigated the computer by keyboard, his hands moving with confidence, guided by memory and intuition. It was a rhythm all his own, as though he had found a language between silence and sound.

Watching him adapt to the new system, Jim felt something close to awe. He realized that independence wasn't always loud or dramatic. Sometimes, it was quiet persistence, the kind that made the impossible look ordinary.

Every morning before sunrise, Jim and Jimmie began their drive from Chicago to Huntley. It was about an hour each way, a small migration that soon became a defining part of their days.

They would leave while the city was still half-asleep. The streets glimmered faintly under streetlights, and the air held that early chill only dawn knows. As they merged onto the highway, the skyline slowly disappeared behind them, replaced by open stretches of land and the low hum of tires on asphalt.

The car became their small, moving world, a quiet place where father and son could talk freely. In those hours, conversation flowed more naturally than it did at home. They spoke about Jimmie's job, their friends, and what lay ahead. Sometimes the topics ran deep; other times, they drifted like soft radio static.

The two hours they spent together each day, one heading out, one coming back, became a kind of daily heartbeat for their relationship. Jim often thought of those drives as a bridge: a suspended space between work and home, between who they were and who they were still becoming.

Jimmie often talked about wanting to live independently one day. He wanted his own place, a life that wasn't defined by his disability. He also spoke of wanting a girlfriend, not someone who would take care of him, but someone who would walk beside him. He wanted partnership, not pity.

Jim listened, proud of the man his son was becoming. There was strength in Jimmie that had nothing to do with vision and everything to do with character.

The factory in Huntley was enormous, 390,000 square feet of machinery, corridors, and organized motion. The air always smelled faintly of metal and oil, and the hum of machines created a rhythm that filled every corner of the building.

When Jimmie started, someone gave him a quick tour, where the reception desk was, the break room, and finally Jim's office. Jim figured it would take time for him to memorize the layout. The building was a maze, after all.

But a few days later, while Jim was finishing paperwork, he heard the familiar, rhythmic tap of a white cane in the hallway. He looked up, and there was Jimmie standing in the doorway, smiling.

"You made it here on your own?" Jim asked, half in disbelief.

"I just remembered," Jimmie said simply.

That moment stayed with Jim for a long time. It was such a small exchange, but it carried the weight of everything a parent hopes for, a moment of realization that his son was finding his own way, literally and metaphorically.

As weeks turned into months, Jimmie settled into the workplace naturally. His coworkers grew to respect and like him, not because of sympathy, but because of his attitude. He worked hard, he listened, and he brought warmth wherever he went.

Jim sometimes watched him from across the room or caught snippets of laughter when Jimmie was talking with someone near reception. Those small sounds meant more to him than most people could imagine.

Jimmie's presence changed how people thought about disability. He didn't lecture or push for recognition, he just lived fully, and by doing so, shifted perspectives without needing to say a word.

The commutes continued, season after season, each one carrying its own rhythm.

In winter, snow would build up along the sides of the highway, and the car heater would hum steadily against the cold. The drive felt longer then, slower, quieter, but they filled it with conversation.

By spring, the fields along the route turned green again, dotted with new construction and the faint shimmer of ponds after rain. Sometimes they rode in silence, the radio murmuring softly, each lost in his own thoughts.

Through it all, those drives became more than routine, they became ritual. A kind of quiet space carved out of their busy lives, where they could connect not as worker and companion, but as equals.

Jim often thought of it as time reclaimed from the noise of life, an hour carved clean, like a straight line through a cluttered map.

He realized, somewhere in those miles, that what he valued most wasn't the job in Huntley or even the professional progress. It was this, these ordinary mornings and evenings, where he could talk to his son without hurry or agenda.

He came to see Jimmie not just as his child, but as his mirror, someone who showed him what resilience really looked like, what quiet courage could do.

The road to Huntley became more than a daily route. It was a thread of understanding, a shared path that stitched together two lives in motion.

Through dark mornings, snowy shoulders, and sunlit afternoons, Jim came to realize that the drive itself was its own kind of education. It wasn't about getting from point A to B anymore. It was about learning to listen, to the hum of the tires, to the steady voice of the man in the seat beside him, and to the quiet truth that sometimes, love doesn't announce itself.

Sometimes, it just rides quietly beside you, mile after mile, on the long road home.

Chapter 25

Even after all the years and the changes, the three of them were still a family, steady in their own orbit, bound by something deeper than daily routines. They still went out to dinner in Chinatown, where the air always smelled faintly of ginger and soy, and the chatter of the restaurants blended with the hiss of steam and clatter of woks. They'd sit by the window with bowls of noodles and dim sum baskets between them, each meal becoming a small celebration of togetherness.

Movies followed the same ritual. The rule was simple: everyone had to agree. It wasn't always easy, but somehow they managed, usually landing somewhere between comedy and drama, something with enough story for Jim, enough heart for Judy, and enough sound for Jimmie to feel the rhythm of the dialogue.

Vacations were still shared, too. They traveled like a unit, three points of a triangle that somehow always found balance. And yet, life had begun to expand beyond that familiar shape.

Jimmie was exploring the world on his own terms now. He and a friend packed up the car one summer and drove down to Florida, chasing the coastline and the salt smell of the ocean. Later, they took a road trip to the Appalachian Mountains, where the air was thinner and the paths twisted through forests that felt older than time. There was something freeing about it, for both him and his parents.

Jim and Judy, meanwhile, started exploring their different corners of the world. They found themselves in Colorado, where the sky looked impossibly wide, and in the cowboy country of the American West, where every diner, dust road, and neon motel seemed to hum with stories of another era.

They laughed their way through Amarillo, where Jimmie, half serious, half joking, had to check his holsters and twin six-shooters at the Cowboy Hall of Fame entrance, earning a few smiles from onlookers. In Cripple Creek, they discovered what Rocky Mountain Oysters really were, to a mixture of horror and amusement.

In Austin, they were measured for cowboy boots, the smell of leather thick in the shop. And in Oklahoma City, they found themselves in one of those roadside attractions that time forgot, posing with a mountain lion on their laps, its calm weight a surreal reminder of how strange and vivid family adventures could be.

Florida called them back again later, not for vacation this time, but for family ties. They stayed in Key Largo, surrounded by the hum of boats, the soft slap of waves against the docks, and evenings that seemed painted in coral light. There, life felt slower, simpler, like time itself had paused to breathe.

But beneath all these shared moments, something quieter was stirring, an undercurrent that comes when life begins to shift directions.

Jim and Judy were both in midlife, that uncertain middle stretch where the road behind you feels longer than the one ahead, and the maps you once relied on no longer quite fit. There wasn't tragedy, not exactly, just a sense of things falling short of expectation.

Jim had returned to the company after a few years in the wider industry. He now held a middle-management position in sales administration: steady, respectable, but not fulfilling. The work paid the bills, but the fire wasn't there. Each day felt slightly smaller than the one before, like a room with the windows slowly closing.

Judy, too, had her own quiet reckoning. The vision she once had of her life, the polished executive's wife, the poised fashion figure, hadn't unfolded as she imagined. Her world had instead settled into something quieter, more modest. She spent her days volunteering at the School of the Art Institute of Chicago, working in the Fashion Resource Center, where famous designers' garments were archived and catalogued. She loved the textures and colors, the stories stitched into each piece of fabric, but sometimes, as she handled a Dior jacket or a Chanel gown, she wondered if she'd missed the life she once dreamed of.

Loss, too, began to weave itself into the edges of their days.

Jim's mother passed away, leaving behind memories that still seemed to echo in his mind at odd hours. Judy's parents divorced, and not long after, both of them died as well, separately, quietly, in the way that life sometimes closes its chapters without ceremony. Then Mother Bennett, Judy's grandmother, passed on too. Each loss added its own layer of heaviness, like clouds gathering slowly, one after another, until the sky dimmed.

It wasn't despair, but it was a season of low light, a kind of gray stretch in their lives that neither could quite name.

In the midst of it all, Jim and Judy tried to mend what had loosened. They traveled, perhaps hoping that distance could unknot what time had tangled. They visited new places, walked beaches, watched sunsets, and told themselves that maybe a change of scenery could shift the undercurrent inside them.

And for a while, it worked. The laughter returned, the silence eased. But each time, as they came home, the feeling faded again, like a photograph left too long in sunlight.

For years, their marriage had revolved around Jimmie: his needs, his achievements, his world. He had been their shared compass, the unspoken purpose that kept them moving in the same direction. But now, with Jimmie stepping confidently into independence, they found themselves standing still, unsure of where to turn next.

They were learning, in their own way, that parenting was a long act of letting go, not just of your child, but of the roles that defined you along the way.

Jim, ever practical, began to search for new purpose. He found comfort in setting goals, in turning uncertainty into something tangible.

Judy was still searching, still trying to define what fulfillment looked like now that the outlines of her life had shifted.

There were evenings when they would sit together in the quiet, the hum of the refrigerator or the faint whistle of wind through the window filling the silence. Neither said much, but there was an understanding between them, an unspoken acknowledgment that love, too, goes through seasons.

Sometimes, it glows bright like the Florida sun. Other times, it fades into the soft gray light of a Chicago afternoon. But even then, it remains, steady, enduring, quietly alive beneath the surface.

They were still a family. That much never changed.

Only now, the shape of that family was beginning to expand, stretching outward, finding new rhythms, and learning to breathe again after years of moving in lockstep.

In their laughter at roadside diners, their quiet drives, and the long silences that didn't need filling, there was something unbreakable still, something that had weathered every storm and still found the strength to stand.

The tides had changed, but they were still together, anchored, not by routine or obligation, but by the invisible thread that had always held them close: love, resilient and quietly certain, even as everything else moved on.

Chapter 26

By the time Jimmie settled into his role in the Human Resources department, he had become a fixture in the building, a quiet, capable presence whose optimism seemed to soften even the most hurried mornings. His colleagues respected him for his professionalism, his humor, and the steady rhythm he brought to the workplace. He'd mastered the adaptive technologies, Braille pads, screen readers, the subtle choreography of keyboard shortcuts, and turned them into tools of independence.

Then came the day when opportunity knocked again. A new position opened at another branch of the company, still within the greater Chicago area, but too far to make the daily drive with his father. It was a step forward: professionally, personally, symbolically. For Jimmie, it wasn't just a transfer; it was a declaration that his world was expanding.

When Jim heard the news, a familiar warmth spread through him, pride mixed with a touch of the ache every parent feels when a child starts moving further into their own orbit. He smiled when Jimmie told him. His son's voice carried that unmistakable brightness, hope wrapped in confidence. Jim could hear it even over the phone line: that light that had never dimmed, even through challenges.

"Sounds like a great move, son," Jim said. "You'll do fine. I know you will."

And Jimmie had already begun to plan his next steps.

He mentioned that one of his high school friends, Eligio, known to everyone as *Hank*, was also getting a new place. The two decided to share an apartment, splitting the rent and the rhythm of their days. It felt right. Hank was solid, dependable, the kind of friend who looked out for others without making it seem like charity. And he'd been part of that trio everyone called *the Three Amigos*, Jimmie, Hank, and Mario.

Mario, the third of the group, was now halfway across the world with the U.S. Navy, sending postcards from distant ports, handwritten notes in bold strokes that carried salt air and freedom between the lines.

That decision, to room with Hank, brought Jim a sense of calm. It was one thing for your son to move out; it was another to know he'd be with someone who knew him, someone who cared.

They found the apartment easily enough. A modern four-story building, not tall by Chicago standards but clean, simple, and filled with the quiet buzz of young professionals coming and going. The building smelled faintly of coffee in the mornings and takeout in the evenings, a living rhythm that seemed to suit Jimmie.

The apartment was about a mile and a half from his new workplace. Close enough that, on good days, he could walk if he wanted, feeling the pavement under his shoes, counting the curbs, memorizing the turns by sound and distance. For him, learning a new route wasn't just logistics, it was the slow claiming of a new world, one sound, one texture, one memory at a time.

Jim helped with the move, carrying boxes labeled in thick black marker: *clothes, records, kitchen, electronics*. Each one felt like a small symbol of independence being unpacked. They furnished the apartment together: a couch that faced the sliding glass doors leading to the balcony, a dining table small enough to be intimate, and the desk where Jimmie's Braille reader and computer setup would sit.

Standing there in the light of the new place, Jim had that same mixed feeling every parent knows, the blend of pride and ache, of wanting to hold on and knowing it's time to let go. The walls were bare, the smell of fresh paint still faint in the air, and outside the window, the Chicago skyline glimmered in the distance.

It wasn't Harbor Point's sweeping view from fifty stories up, but it was his own. And that mattered more.

The building had balconies on each floor, separated by narrow partitions of brick and metal railings. It was the kind of modern design that looked uniform from the street, each unit identical in size and shape, but inside, life unfolded differently in every one.

One morning, Hank accidentally locked the apartment door with the keys still inside. A small, ordinary mistake, one that could happen to anyone. But for Jimmie, it could have meant being stuck.

Except he wasn't the type to wait helplessly.

When the neighbor offered to let him out onto their balcony, Jimmie took the chance. With quiet focus and unshakable courage, he gripped the railing, swung one leg over, and felt his way around the narrow divider, inch by inch, forty feet above the ground.

When Jim later heard the story, he could only shake his head in disbelief and awe. "Not bad for a handicapped guy," he said, half laughing, half terrified at the thought. "Not something I'd ever try."

It was pure Jimmie, fearless, determined, refusing to be limited by anyone's idea of what was possible.

Evenings at the apartment had their own rhythm. The hum of the refrigerator, the occasional knock from the neighbor's door, the scent of microwave popcorn. Jimmie and Hank often spent their nights with movies from Blockbuster, that blue-and-yellow symbol of 1980s entertainment.

Jim sometimes wondered how his son, who couldn't see, could find joy in a medium so visual. But Jimmie had a way of "watching" that defied expectation. He absorbed dialogue, tone, silence, the spaces between words. He remembered the cadence of every actor's voice, the rhythm of background music, the way laughter or footsteps filled a scene.

Movies, for him, weren't pictures, they were worlds of sound.

Over time, he became a regular at the local rental store. The clerks knew him by name and would describe the new releases, summarizing plots and reading out taglines. He'd ask questions, curious, engaged, always interested in how the business ran.

And that curiosity grew into an idea.

One evening, after work, he sat down with his father and said, "Dad, what if I opened a video store? One of my own."

Jim blinked, a little caught off guard, but Jimmie was already outlining the plan, how it could work, how it could serve both sighted and visually impaired customers, how it could be marketed. "Think about it," he said, smiling. "Imagine the headline… 'Blind Man Opens Video Store.' It'd be good for business, and maybe even for others like me."

He'd already written a business plan, typed neatly with Braille notations at the edge of each page.

Jim read through it that night, equal parts impressed and moved. The idea wasn't just ambitious, it was bold, and it showed Jimmie's spirit in full. He told his son he'd think about investing, not because he doubted him, but because he wanted to make sure they could do it right.

And as he drove home that night, Jim couldn't help but smile. His son's dreams had always been bigger than any obstacle in front of him.

That evening, he decided to stop by one of his old college fraternity brothers' homes to talk over the business idea. They'd share a drink, run through the numbers, maybe sketch out the next steps.

Jimmie had called earlier, sounding a little under the weather. "I've got a bit of a cold," he'd said lightly. "Just staying home tonight."

"Alright," Jim had replied. "Get some rest. I'll stop by tomorrow."

Those were the last words he'd hear from him.

Later that night, as Jim was heading home, his phone rang. The voice on the other end was shaky, Hank's voice.

"Mr. Jim," he said, breathless. "I just got home from work. I checked on Jimmie. He… he wasn't responding. I called 911. They're taking him to the hospital."

The world seemed to blur around the edges. Jim didn't remember hanging up or starting the car, just the hum of the engine and the pounding of his heart. He drove through the Chicago night, every traffic light a blur, every turn a silent prayer.

Please, God. Not this. Not him. Please.

He prayed out loud, the words tumbling and repeating, his voice breaking. The city outside his windshield was a smear of color, red lights, streetlamps, the dark outlines of buildings that felt suddenly colder than he'd ever known.

By the time he reached the hospital, the night air was still, the fluorescent lights too bright. He rushed through the doors, the smell of antiseptic heavy in the air, the sound of footsteps echoing on tile.

A nurse met him, her expression was soft, practiced. It was the look of someone who had delivered this kind of news before.

She led him to a quiet room.

And there, with the weight of her words, the world fell silent.

Jimmie was gone.

Just like that, the heartbeat of their family, the laughter, the music, the plans, all fell into stillness.

Jim stood there, unable to move, unable to breathe. The prayers he had whispered on the drive were still on his lips, unanswered. The silence that filled that hospital room was vast, like standing at the edge of an ocean after the tide has gone out, and all that remains is the sound of your own breathing.

In the days that followed, the world seemed to move in slow motion. The apartment still smelled faintly of Jimmie's cologne, the faint scent of fabric softener from the laundry he'd done that week. His things were where he left them, the Braille reader, the desk chair slightly pushed back, the stack of Blockbuster tapes beside the television.

The balcony door was closed, but the light from outside cast a golden stripe across the floor, just as it always had.

Neighbors stopped by, quiet, unsure of what to say. Hank spoke softly, retelling the moment he found his friend, his voice catching in the middle of every sentence.

Jim listened, but the words passed through him like wind through a hollow space. He was grateful, and broken, and still trying to understand how a life so full of courage and laughter could be gone so suddenly.

There are moments that divide time, *before* and *after*.

For Jim, that night was the line that split his world in two.

Before: mornings filled with conversation in the car, laughter over coffee, dreams about a video store, plans for next summer.

After: silence, the absence of footsteps, and the hollow ache of a future that no longer existed.

And yet, even in grief, there was something unmistakable, a light that refused to go out. Jimmie's spirit lingered in every memory, every echo of laughter that came unbidden, every time the sun hit the water on a clear Chicago morning.

Jim would often stand by the window of their high-rise, looking out at the lake where they once sailed, watching how the light moved across the waves. And sometimes, when the wind hit just right, he swore he could still hear his son's voice, steady, calm, and full of life.

"Trim the sail, Dad," it seemed to say. "Adjust your course. The wind's still good."

And though the world had changed, Jim knew that somewhere, somehow, that same wind carried Jimmie forward, into a horizon unseen but forever illuminated.

Chapter 27

What do we do now?

The words still circle in my head, soft at first, then heavier each time they return. They don't sound like a question anymore, more like a pulse, a rhythm beneath everything, steady and merciless. *What do we do now?* It lives inside the walls, under the hum of the refrigerator, inside the ticking of the clock that hasn't stopped since the day the world did.

The house feels cavernous. Every sound is too loud, every silence too complete. The air carries a stillness I can't get used to, a weight pressing against the chest, making even breathing an effort. What do we do now, when the house is too quiet, when every photo on the wall has turned into a ghost?

Our parents are gone. Our grandparents are gone. Our only child is gone. And I am left here, stranded in the middle of all that silence, a man who has outlived every generation that once gave him shape, every voice that once called his name. The world has thinned somehow. The color has faded out of it, leaving behind only outlines of what used to be real.

There are mornings when I wake too early, caught between dreaming and waking, and for a few seconds, just a few, everything feels whole again. I can almost hear Jimmie's voice calling out from the hallway, light and cheerful, like he used to when he wanted to know what was for breakfast. Sometimes it's laughter that reaches me first, that open, bright sound that used to fill this place like sunlight. And sometimes it's quieter: the faint rattle of his cane tapping against the doorframe, the rhythm so familiar it feels etched into my bones.

Once, I swear I smelled coffee brewing, strong and dark, the way he liked it when he thought he was being grown-up. I smiled before I even opened my eyes. But when I did, the air was empty. Just the curtains moving in the half-light, the wind brushing them gently, like a hand that wants to touch but can't quite reach.

That's how grief feels most days, a touch that never lands, a voice that never finishes the sentence. I lie there sometimes, staring at the ceiling, and let the ache spread through me, slow and deliberate, the way ink seeps into paper. It doesn't hurt sharply anymore. It just fills me, quietly, endlessly, until I am made of it.

Some mornings, I don't move at all. I listen. I listen to the house breathe. I listen for the memory of him, the way he moved through the rooms, the way his laughter found its way into everything, even the dullest corners. I used to think memories were kind. Now I know they're cleverer than that, they know exactly when to appear, when to slip under the skin and remind you that time doesn't heal; it just rearranges the pain into something you can carry without breaking every minute.

The pictures on the wall have become a kind of mirror. I look at them and see ghosts of movement, gestures half-alive. His smile stares back at me from behind the glass, unaging, untouched, forever seventeen, forever alive in a world that keeps moving without him. The photos no longer comfort me; they haunt me. They whisper, *We were here once. We were real once.*

And maybe that's what life becomes after loss, a long conversation with the invisible. I speak to him sometimes, softly, like I'm afraid to disturb the air. I tell him about the weather, about the small things, the birds on the balcony, the mail that keeps coming, the days that refuse to stop arriving. I tell him I miss him, though I know he already knows. And then I listen.

There's never an answer, not in words. But sometimes, when the morning light hits the wall just right, I feel something, a warmth, a flicker, a pulse, as if love, once given, never truly leaves.

And then the silence folds back around me, and the day begins again.

A few months after Jimmie died, I lost my job. Thirty-three years, gone in a single meeting that lasted less than an hour. I remember walking out into the parking lot, the world spinning like it didn't care who had just fallen out of it. Fifty-five years old, jobless, childless, carrying grief like it was another organ inside me, something I couldn't remove, only live around.

I didn't cry then. I didn't even speak. I just drove back to Harbor Point and sat in the garage for what felt like forever, watching the sunlight fade across the dashboard.

When I finally went upstairs and opened the door to our unit, Judy was there. I could see the fear in her eyes, the same one that's lived in mine since we lost him. I told her what happened, and she just nodded. No tears, no anger. We'd already spent them all.

So we did what we always did, we worked. We built something out of the ashes.

Valentines Enterprises Ltd. Two people, a dream, a lifeline disguised as a business. I was president, she was vice-president, though titles meant nothing between us. Our lawyer asked how we'd handle board decisions and suggested "unanimous consent." I laughed, a dry sound, half memory, half exhaustion, and said, *"That's perfect. If Judy doesn't want to do it, we won't."* That's how we'd always lived, in agreement, in quiet survival.

The company did well, almost miraculously so. The first month, we earned more than my last salary. It should have felt triumphant. But all I could think was how proud Jimmie would have been. He would've called it "Dad's comeback." I could almost hear him say it, teasingly, his smile audible in the words.

But he wasn't there. And every success was lined with absence, every invoice, every phone call, every small victory.

We poured ourselves into that company. It wasn't about money. It was about distraction, about filling the unbearable silence with something that resembled purpose. We had to keep moving, or the grief would catch us. It always did, anyway. Sometimes it came quietly, a smell, a song, a phrase someone used. Sometimes it came like a wave that crushed the breath out of us.

At first, those waves came every hour. Then every day. Then, slowly, they began to stretch apart, a week, a month, maybe two. But they never disappeared. They just changed shape.

That's the thing no one tells you about grief: it doesn't fade, it rearranges itself. It waits behind ordinary moments, the clink of silverware, the closing of a door, and when you least expect it, it steps forward and reminds you that love has nowhere else to go.

Holidays were the worst. Weddings, Christmas, birthdays.

We learned to avoid them when we could. Family gatherings were traps of memory, too many faces, too many questions, too many empty chairs.

When we couldn't avoid them, we survived by hugging. A hug is a strange thing, so simple, but it saved us more than once. When words were too painful, a hug spoke what we couldn't say: *We're still here. We still remember. We still love him.*

Christmas was unbearable.

We started booking cruises, two weeks at sea, just the two of us, where no one knew us as parents, only as a couple. On those ships, we were anonymous. We were allowed to exist without pity. We spent Christmas Eve watching the ocean turn silver under the moon, the horizon endless and merciful. I used to imagine Jimmie somewhere beyond that horizon, sailing too, maybe laughing at our attempt to outrun grief.

But time, that quiet healer, did what it does best. It didn't erase the pain, but it softened the edges. The sharpness dulled into something almost tender. I began to speak of Jimmie again, first in small mentions, then in stories, and now in this, in these pages that hold him like light caught in glass.

There are still days when it feels like he's just gone for a while, maybe out sailing, maybe walking home. I think about his bravery, the way he navigated a world that wasn't built for him, how he never asked for sympathy, how he made every obstacle seem temporary. He climbed balconies forty feet in the air without sight, opened doors that others assumed were closed to him, and taught me what courage looked like without ever saying the word.

Sometimes, late at night, I walk to the window and look out over the city. The lights flicker in the distance, little fires against the dark. I think about all the lives still being lived, all the love still fighting to exist despite everything.

And I whisper his name. Not because I expect an answer, but because saying it keeps him here. Keeps *me* here.

If grief is love with nowhere to go, then maybe this, these words, this remembering, is how I give it somewhere to rest.

He is in every part of me now. In the quiet mornings. In the laughter I still find with Judy. In the moments of stillness that used to terrify me but now simply ache.

I used to ask, *What do we do now?*

Now I know. We live. We build. We remember.

We carry the love forward, not as a burden, but as proof that he was here, that we were a family, that love outlasts everything.

And when the waves come, as they still do, I don't fight them anymore. I let them wash over me, because in their weight, I find him again.

That's how I survive. That's how I keep him alive.

Not in the past, not in memory alone, but in the quiet act of continuing.

In the small, steady rhythm of breath that still insists on being taken.

In the echo of his laughter that still lingers in the corners of my mind.

In the story I now tell, our story, so the world will know that Jimmie lived, that he was loved beyond measure, and that love, when it is true, never dies.

About the Author

Jim Valentine, born in Chicago in 1938, served in the Army after graduating from Knox College in 1961. He worked at Union Special Machine Company, holding various management roles across the U.S., Canada, and Latin America. Jim and his family moved multiple times, living in Germany, Boston, Worth, and New York before settling in Chicago.

In 1993, Jim retired from Union Special and founded Valentine Enterprises, relocating to Fort Lauderdale in 2007. After 31 successful years as a business owner, he sold his company in 2024. Jim was a community leader, serving as president of the Junior Chamber of Commerce. Jim was also named president of the Chicago Knox College Club, president of the Knox College Alumni Association, president and founder of the Siwash Athletic Club, and recipient of the Knox College Service Award for exemplary service.

Jim also enjoys playing golf and has a great passion for cars.